I0724944

RELIQUARY

NOVELLA

AMANDA BOOLOODIAN

DEDICATION

Thank you for your patience while waiting for this novella to be released!

CONTENTS

CHAPTER
ONE

The box shook in Gran's hand and I almost stepped back. Her ex may have good intentions, at least when it came to Gran, but the man was crazier than a drunk pixie.

"He wouldn't give you anything dangerous, would he?" I asked.

"What a thing to say." Gran carefully sat the package on the kitchen table. "It's supposed to keep us safe, so it has to be deadly. He said we need to open it together."

I bit my lip, but went to stand beside her.

Boone cast a wary glance our way. "Should I be here?"

"Of course you should," Gran said. "Your breakfast will turn cold if you leave."

Boone grinned, but eyed the box. After being trapped in another world with me, he was familiar with the type of help the old man gave.

Gran pried open the lid, and we both leaned forward for a better look at her present.

I blinked at the contents, nonplussed. "It's a kitten."

Boone attempted to peer inside, but tried to hide it, which meant he saw nothing.

The cat peeked up at me and Gran, then reached out its front legs and stretched.

My eyes widened as wings ruffled out on either side of the creature.

"If that's a cat, mine have been keeping some big secrets." Gran reached her hand in and scratched the animal behind its ears, then took off a piece of paper fastened to our package.

"Brrrr," the animal trilled.

My heart bubbled up, so I couldn't help but hold out my hand to allow the furry bundle to tentatively sniff. I wanted to do was pick up the tiny animal, but I was still leery about a creature given to us by Gran's ex, so I settled on scratching behind the ears.

"It's called an ichneu," Gran said. "I've never actually seen one before--thought they were extinct. Hughes has talked about them, of course."

"So, your ex bought you a pet?" I asked.

"She's much more than that. Come on, let's show her the house."

Gran must have looked more closely than I did to notice the ichneu was female.

"We'll be back," I said, nodding to Boone as we left the room.

"Aren't you adorable," Gran added to the ichneu as she took the box into the living room and then picked the creature up. The little animal appeared tiny in Gran's hands and with its wings tucked away she looked like the kitten I had mistaken her for.

"What do you think of the name Molly?" Gran asked.

"Brrrr?"

"I think she likes the name," I said, grinning involuntarily.

"Molly it is, then," Gran said. "Come on, Molly, we're going to show you your new home."

About halfway through the tour, Gran passed Molly to me. The ichneu had beautiful white fur with black markings around the eyes. Her wings disappeared seamlessly into the sides of her body until she shifted or stretched.

"Why are we showing her around?" I asked. "Not that I mind."

"She needs to know what she's in charge of." Gran unfolded the note. "She'll attack anyone in her territory unless we introduce them to her."

"We're going to have quite a few scratched ankles around the house."

Gran chuckled. "She'll grow bigger. Ichneu were dragon killers."

I looked at the tiny ball of fur in my arms as we re-entered the kitchen.

Molly noticed Boone for the first time. She screeched and clawed at me, trying to break free.

"You calm down right now, young lady," Gran said. "Mr. Boone, you hold your hand out for her to smell and you all will become fast friends."

Restraining Molly while she growled deep in her throat made me a little nervous. Boone mirrored the sentiment, but he held out his hand, albeit cautiously.

"Molly," Gran said, "this is Boone. Play nice with him."

Molly sniffed a few times then appeared bored with Boone, so we moved on.

As we showed her the kitchen Gran's cat entered and Molly froze in my hands. The old tom was more than four times larger than Molly, but he was the closest thing to her size that she'd seen.

Holding on to Molly, I squatted down next to Gran's cat. He

didn't particularly like me, but he looked intrigued by Molly. The two tentatively touched noses and after Molly began to purr I sat her down. Once they met the old tom didn't seem impressed. Gran's cat sauntered out of the room and Molly trotted closely behind.

"You have an attack cat," Boone said as I sat down.

I couldn't help but grin. "She's not a cat." He was right, though, that's what Gran's beau had given her.

The doorbell rang followed by the front door opening.

"It is me," Rider called.

Boone grinned. "Let's see what your new girl--"

A loud yowl cut Boone off.

The clatter that went through the house sounded much larger than any one little animal should be able to create.

Rider walked into the kitchen, looking worriedly at the creature wrapped around his leg.

I jumped up and pulled Molly off her prey. "Rider, I'm sorry, she drew blood."

"What is it?" Rider asked.

I introduced the pair. As soon as Molly formally met Rider, she was okay with him, but remained curious.

"She is going to guard the house?" Rider asked.

"Accordin' to the paper she came with, she's going to double in size in the next few weeks," Gran said. "After that growth spurt, she'll stay the same for a while, and then she'll grow again."

"How big will she get?" I asked.

"Who knows," Gran said. "But I feel safer with her around already."

"It still might be better if I moved out," I said, not really liking the idea. Gran made a wonderful roommate, but the scarier parts of my job kept following me home.

"I won't hear of it," Gran said. "Now eat your breakfast. Rider, take a seat. Are you sure you should even be awake?"

Not only had Rider been here until late in the night, but he had also been injured recently. My own wounds, especially the cuts on my arm, had started to itch--a sure sign of healing.

"I am well," Rider said. "I wished they would not put a cast like this on. Will I get into trouble if I tear it off?"

"You don't take a cast off, a doctor does," I said.

"I have healed. The only thing the plaster is doing is making my arm hot and itchy."

"We'll get someone to look at it soon," I said. "You haven't heard from Vincent yet, have you?"

Molly had distracted me for more than an hour. With that diversion over, there was only one thing occupying my mind.

"I have not," Rider said. "I am sure he will call when he is able."

The words really didn't sink in. Vincent's sudden absence left a gaping hole in my heart. Last night I tossed and turned, wondering where he was, what was happening to him, and if he was okay.

Telling myself I was being pathetic didn't help. We only shared a kiss the previous day, nothing else, and there hadn't been a chance to discuss what that meant.

But it was a kiss with Vincent. My Vincent.

At least I thought he was mine.

I hoped he was.

All this floated through my mind for the thousandth time, and with my thoughts turned inward, I almost missed the conversation around me.

"You are leaving?" Rider asked.

"This afternoon," Boone said.

"I didn't realize you'd be taking off so soon," I said.

"The attack by the changeling has something to do with

the project I'm being assigned. I need to get started before there are any new surprises."

I gave him a weak smile. "Your whole visit has been one surprise after another."

"I'm sure you could do with a few less of them," Boone said.

"If the excitement stayed in this world, it wouldn't be so bad," I said.

"Well, the last week has been educational," Boone said. "Next time we get together, let's stick to the office."

I grinned. "You remember what happened at the office, right?"

Boone chuckled. "When the bad guys come calling it's better to meet them at the office than have them turn up here or take us to another world."

"True. Do you need a ride?" I asked.

"I'm meeting Logan at his house." Boone got up and rinsed off his plate. "He's giving me a lift."

"Rider, will you help me with somethin'?" Gran asked.

"Of course."

They left and Boone and I found ourselves alone.

"I'm sorry about Vincent," Boone said.

"He'll be back," I said with forced optimism. "It may take him a while, but he'll make it."

"It's been interesting working with you."

"Same here."

We stood awkwardly, knowing something should be said, but having no clue how to say it.

"I'm not good at this," I admitted.

He grinned. "Me neither. Thanks for getting us back."

"Thanks for keeping us alive."

"There wouldn't have been a need if I hadn't been here in the first place."

I shook my head. "We can't blame ourselves for what the crazies do. I'm just glad I had the chance to meet you and work with you."

"I'm not sure how long I'll be tied up with this new project. When it's over, I may see about coming back to the area."

"That'd be great. And wherever you're going, if you need a hand with anything... well, I'm probably not much help, but if you call me, I'll do what I can. We all will."

Boone chuckled. "You sell yourself short. I've seen what you can do."

My power as a Reader allowed me to read traces left by anything moving through our world. It was the only thing that made me useful as an investigator. After a failed assassination attempt, my power grew substantially, allowing me to not only see the overlaying Path, but manipulate it as well.

"Speaking of," Boone continued, "how's your head?"

I self-consciously rubbed my forehead and looked away, thinking of my disastrous attempts at using my power the day before and the consequences that followed . "It stopped pounding sometime early this morning. I'm not sure what I did, but Taylor might be able to figure it out."

"He's the MyTH doctor, right?"

"Yeah, they won't let me go back to work yet, so I'm going to spend some time in the city."

Boone nodded. "I should head to the office in case they need me for anything before my flight."

"Don't run off too quickly," Gran said, bustling in and going straight to the counter, where several bags had been left out. Rider came in behind her, looking confused. "Mr. Boone, since you're on your way over, take this to Logan and the kids." She handed off a plastic bag packed to bursting with cookies inside.

"I wish we had met under better circumstances," Rider

said, shaking hands with Boone. "But I enjoyed working with you."

"And these are for you." Gran said, handing Boone another bag with cookies and brownies inside. "A thank you for taking care of my granddaughter. Now, hide them in your bag or Gerald will have them out of your sight before you even notice he's there."

When Boone's hands were full, Gran hugged him. "You come on back here when you can."

And with that, Boone grabbed his bag and walked out the back door.

"Wait," Gran called.

Boone stepped back inside and closed the door again, glancing down in case our pets wanted to make a break for it.

Gran had a faraway look in her eyes. "Don't be afraid to reach out if you need anything. Cassie can help."

Boone raised an eyebrow at me, and I shrugged.

"I'll remember that," Boone said. "Thank you again."

Then he was gone. After spending so much time with him, it felt strange to know he wouldn't be around when I woke up tomorrow.

"Darlin'," Gran said, "take some aspirin now, you're gonna need it."

"Oh? Why?" I tried not to groan. My head had been splitting yesterday, and I didn't want to face the same again today.

"Hard to say, but you'll want it. Dee Dee will be picking me up shortly. Don't forget your gun. You might need that too."

"This doesn't sound like a promising day. Maybe I should go back to bed."

"You're supposed to meet up with that cute doctor of yours. You may as well start packing now."

"I didn't think we'd be getting together until tomorrow."

"I don't think you should wait," Gran said. "You need to be in the city."

The idea of leaving so quickly didn't sit well with me. "I'm not sure this is the best time to go."

"Molly will take care of any trouble. Besides, I may want to have a guest over while you're gone." Gran winked at me.

"Oh." The last thing I wanted to do was be in Gran's way, but I still didn't think it was the best idea to leave the day after someone broke into our home. "I guess then..."

"And your mother will be here this evenin'. Don't you worry, Gerald and Susan are across the yard. I'll call them if I see anything I can't handle. Besides," she patted her purse, "I'm ready this time."

"Be careful with that thing." Sweet little old lady that she appeared, she'd have no problem holding back a normal intruder with the gun she kept with her. But a Lost? "You'll call me if you need anything?"

"Of course, darlin'. You go with your friends."

I had to admit, it was better than staying at home and worrying about Vincent; besides, if I wasn't home, no bad guys would come, right?

"I should pack," Rider said after Gran left the room.

"If you don't mind waiting a few minutes, I'll go with you."

"If you are sure," Rider said. "I can come back to pick you up."

"No, I'll go with you." I didn't say the words aloud, but I didn't want to be alone in the house. Earlier that morning I found myself staring at the spot where Vincent disappeared.

Once I finished the dishes I dashed upstairs and I packed a bunch of clothes, but a squeal slowed my process. I wasn't quite sure about what to do with Frank. Vincent watched him while I had been trapped in another world, and now I was running off without a plan for the rabbit.

Well, Taylor had always been interested in my zombie bunny. After I packed I grabbed his cage and hurried downstairs.

Rider was doing the same thing I had been that morning, staring at the place where Vincent left our world.

"Does it smell odd where he crossed over?" I asked in a lowered voice. I wasn't sure I wanted to know the answer.

"It does not. His trail simply vanishes," Rider said.

"I really wish he was still here."

"Me too. I have much to discuss with him. I am happy that the two of you got together before he went away."

"I'm not sure we're a couple or anything," I admitted. "We didn't really get the chance to talk about it."

"In this case, I do not think there is need for discussion. You two belong together."

"We've never had the chance to discuss it. I was seeing Ethan, and before that Vincent took a different monster between the worlds to save us, but he didn't let me know he was back. Running back into him had been a chance accident." Saying that made me even more paranoid. *He would come back, right?*

"He will return sooner this time," Rider said as though he read my mind. "Then I will know if he wants me to stay or leave."

Another uncomfortable subject. While I was trapped in the gremlin world, Rider had had the briefest of thoughts that his life might be easier if I didn't come back. The entire incident was a huge cultural misunderstanding, but my heart turned heavy when I thought about it.

"Like I said before, you can't help what you think some-times. Besides, I've forgiven you--he'll have to do the same." I left the house hoping to spur a change in subject.

"Have you?" Rider asked.

"We discussed this. I understood why--"

"Understanding and forgiving are two different things."

"I forgive you." I tried to give him a reassuring smile. "Don't worry about what Vincent will say. He'll get over it."

Rider nodded, but didn't appear convinced. "How is your arm?"

"Besides my skin being held together by thread?" I shivered at the thought. "It's surprisingly not bad. How's yours?"

"It is healed."

"Good, then you can drive," I said, hoisting up Frank's cage into Rider's truck while Rider grabbed my bag.

Once we were ensconced in Rider's over-sized vehicle, I called Logan. It was more to take my mind off Rider's driving than anything else.

"Howdy," Logan said.

"Morning," I said. "How are things at the office?"

"Things aren't going so great here. I'm glad you reached me. You need to turn off your phone."

"I do?"

"It wouldn't hurt if Rider did as well. Put them in one of those pouches I gave you."

Logan had gifted each of us a bag that blocked all signals. He never openly said he thought work was spying on us or tracking our movements, but he certainly acted like it.

Him being worried about our devices now made me nervous. "What's going on?"

"Let's just say there's some out-of-towners coming in and they sound real interested in talking to you. All of us, really."

"Paulson has our statements."

"Hank seemed to think they want to know more about Vincent."

"What? Why?"

"Because he's disappeared."

"But that's what he does," I reminded Logan.

"Hank said they didn't seem to be happy with that."

"I can't turn off my phone."

"Why not?"

"Because he might call."

Logan sighed. "I'll see if there's something Hank can do."

"Rider and I were on our way out of town to visit Taylor. Do you think I should stay."

"Don't. Go, and I'll join ya."

Once Logan disconnected, the only thing to concentrate on was Vincent's lack of contact and Rider's cavalier approach to traffic. Rider swooped in front of a semi in order to make his exit, causing his driving to jump into the forefront of my thoughts.

When Rider was young he had lived in this world, his mother passed away, leaving him her house. His father took Rider back to his own world. When forced to leave the home world of the werewolves, Rider decided to return to this one.

We met shortly after he moved back to the little country house. Within a few days of meeting we'd become friends and I considered myself very lucky to have him here.

"You've done some landscaping," I mentioned as I jumped down from his truck.

"I needed to keep busy," Rider said.

"I guess it's been a while since I've been out here."

"It has. Come inside. I will not take long."

In Rider's living room I gravitated to a tree--at least, it appeared to be one. In reality it was the Path--something only a Reader could see--pulled into the normal world and made solid. The object was something I made by accident. In its original form it was a beautiful, but obviously alien substance. Gerald, Logan's youngest, was an extremely talented painter, and when Gerald finished his work, my creation was so realistic as a tree that it could easily be mistaken for a living plant.

"How long do you think we will be gone?" Rider called from his bedroom deeper in the house.

"I have no idea," I admitted. "But I packed for a week."

When I created the tree it had been magnificent, but who knew what time would to do pure raw Path in the real world? Since paint covered the piece there was no way to tell by looking, but I had another way to check.

I closed my eyes and stretched my mind out. Once I reached the end of the knowledge of everything I knew, I made the leap and jumped straight into the Path. For one moment I saw the outline of my work, just as strong and stunning as it was when it first formed.

Then I screamed.

Fiery rivers of Path scorched across my brain. I clutched my head in a vain attempt to damn the flow, but it burned too hot and too bright.

Something brushed past me and I turned. Power scalded my veins. A hint of a shadow stood in the corner by the tree.

It was a figure.

A hand gripped my arm and I screamed again, wrenching away. As I jerked back, my leg hit the couch at an odd angle and I fell to the floor.

Before the fiery Path could boil my blood, I gritted my teeth and drove the Path away. Instantly, my body began to cool. When I felt able, I focused on my creation again, but it stood alone. Rider squatted not far away, though, radiating concern.

I pushed myself up to a sitting position and rubbed my temples. Although the heat dissipated, a shadowy memory of the Path beat itself against my mind.

The tears running down my face weren't a surprise. They dried fast as the pain receded, so I wiped away the remnants.

"I am not sure what happened," Rider said.

A bark of laughter burst out of me. "You and me both."

"Tell me."

I shook my head, unsure about what to say.

"Is it because you are near the tree?" Rider asked.

"No, it started yesterday, when I tried to stop the changeling. My soul was whole, but... pliable. I broke through, which shattered my essence a second time."

"And your power is different now?" Rider asked.

"It seems that way."

"How so?"

"It's like pumping boiling water through my body."

"That does not sound safe. Did it feel worse when I touched your arm?" He looked as though he struggled to understand.

"No, you didn't hurt me or anything," I rushed to explain. "There was..." I glanced up at the tree. There couldn't have been something standing there. Not really. "You startled me, is all," I ended lamely.

"You are not saying something."

He knew me too well. "I need some time to process."

He didn't seem happy about it, but it appeared he would accept the explanation. At least for now.

What else could I say, though? 'There are shapes in the Path with me?' Traces were always around when I read. I could say someone bushed against me, but that sounded... crazy. It was ludicrous, even to myself. I had been in contact with another Reader, and if she told me we weren't alone in the Path, I wouldn't believe her.

Even after seeing the figure, I didn't accept the idea. This wasn't like Fenrir--a wolf that could move in and out of the Path--this was different. It felt as though the Path was haunted.

I shivered at the thought.

"I'm okay now," I said, moving to sit on the couch instead of the floor.

Rider remained nearby and seemed to be thinking hard.

"It's just new," I tried to reassure him. Too bad no one was around to convince me of the same. "I'll adjust."

"Maybe you should not use your power."

I stared at him blankly. He may as well have been asking me to chop off an arm. When my powers had weakened to the point I could barely see the Path, it was as though the sun no longer shone. I had been prepared to learn to live with that—I wasn't sure I could adapt to the new issues, but not reading at all wasn't an option.

"I don't think I need to go that far," I said.

"If you are causing yourself damage, you need to stop."

"Nothing physically is happening. I'm sure it's not, otherwise the effects would continue after I stopped reading." I realized I was still rubbing my temple and forced my hand away from my head.

"Let us see what Taylor has to say. As your doctor, he will be able to see if it has harmed you."

"I'll talk to him about it when we see him," I said. "Why don't you finish getting ready."

Rider nodded and rose to his feet. "It will only take me a few minutes." He stood so tall in the little house that it seemed he should brush against the ceiling. That only happened when he went through doorways, though. "You should call Taylor."

I wrinkled up my nose, but didn't argue. After Rider left the room, however, I stalled. Looking at the tree without checking the Path, it appeared to be a normal plant. Was the figure standing next to it also made of Path?

Had there been anything there? Maybe the agony of reading made me hallucinate.

Wait, is that any better?

Sighing inwardly, I took out my phone and called Taylor.

"Cassie," he said, answering on the first ring, "I was going to check in with you before I left, but I was needed at MyTH."

"I take it things are caught up at the Farm?" I asked.

"Dr. Yelton said he could manage the rest. Since AIR has some people coming in from out of town, your office thought it would be better if I wasn't at the Farm when they arrived. I'm not an agent, after all."

"It's funny, I *am* an agent and received very similar advice."

Rider came out and we went to the car while Taylor and I continued the discussion.

"It's good timing for me, then," Taylor said. "Would you all be available to come into the city for a few days?"

"We're already on our way," I said. "That's why I was calling. Logan won't be joining us until later, though."

"Then I'm doubly lucky," Taylor said. "We could use your team here."

"Gran said you'd need us."

"It's certainly better that it doesn't wait. How is your grandmother doing today?"

"She's well. She was going out with Dee Dee when I left."

"That's good. How about you?"

I cast a sideways glance at Rider. "I'm alright, but there are a few things I wanted to talk with you about when we meet."

"Logan mentioned the headaches yesterday. I'll be able to run some tests here in the clinic."

"Speaking of which, I brought Frank along as well."

"Oh!" Taylor's voice seemed to light up. "He is such an interesting animal. I'd love to examine him and see how he's doing."

"Are there rooms free at the office?" I asked.

"We're empty of guests at the moment. I'm certain MyTH can keep you busy for as long as you need. Besides, Logan and

Jonathan will get a chance to spend some time with each other, which will be good for both of them."

I smiled and we exchanged our goodbyes.

When I glanced up, I saw Rider manically weaving in and out of traffic, so I distracted myself by staring at my phone. Logan's warning to put my cell away in the signal blocking case came to mind. Since Vincent could call at any time there was no chance I'd cut off any lines of communication.

Honestly, though, I didn't think he'd call soon. It would take a leprechaun for me to be lucky enough to hear from him in even a few days.

Somehow, I still held out a wisp of hope, so I counted on Hank to make something work. I'm sure Logan wouldn't go into the city without telling our handler where he was going.

"Logan suggested we put away our phones. Do you want me to take yours?" I asked Rider.

"I thought about adding it to my case, but I would not like to do so."

He didn't have to say why.

"Me either," I said.

"He will be back."

I wasn't sure if he was trying to convince himself or me, so I said nothing.

MyTH stood for the Mythological Terrestrial Humanitarians. The man who started the organization had once been an AIR Agent, but the bureaucracy meant he couldn't help the Lost, mythological creatures from other dimensions, in the way he wanted. Now, MyTH runs in the private sector and picks up where AIR leaves off.

At the agency, we find the Lost, keep their secret safe, and relocate them. MyTH assists the Lost on a continuing basis. If I ever left AIR, I'd hope to find a job with MyTH. Their offices crisscrossed the country, but the closest location was in the city, where Taylor worked. The building was unassuming. What few windows they had were dark and impossible to see into, which was good because the office wasn't in the best neighborhood in town.

Taylor met us at the door, handing over temporary security passes so we could come and go as we wanted.

"I'll show you to your rooms, and you can get Frank settled in," Taylor said.

"Thanks for letting us stay," I said. "What's been going on that you need help with?"

"First things first," he said. "I've got an MRI machine waiting for you."

The idea made me uncomfortable. "That seems excessive."

"Not at all."

"Gran said your problem couldn't wait."

Taylor hesitated. "Did she say *seeing me* couldn't wait or my problem couldn't wait?"

"I... I'm not sure. I don't think she was that specific."

"Then we start with the MRI."

I dropped my stuff off in the room I had stayed in before and sat Frank's cage on the dresser. When I fed him a leaf of lettuce the rabbit made a few contented squeaks before settling in.

The hallways at MyTH were virtually silent as Rider and I went to the clinic.

"Where's Neil?" I asked Taylor when we arrived.

Taylor cringed slightly. "He's in his lab. Supposedly he's cleaning it, but I don't think he knows what that means."

I chuckled. Neil was the smartest person I had ever known, yet a complete idiot at the same time. Especially when it came to drugs. He self-medicated to dumb himself down.

"And Jonathan?" I asked.

"He's on assignment but should be stopping by later tonight to visit his dad. When does Logan get in?"

I shrugged. "I'm not sure. He may have turned off his phone."

"Really?" Taylor said.

"He doesn't want the office to track us, I think," I said.

"Are you all in some sort of trouble?" Taylor asked.

I shook my head, but said nothing.

"Vincent is gone," Rider said. "Two agents, one of them being Cassie, were recently pushed into another world and trapped. I think there is some worry we've done the same to Vincent."

My mouth dropped open. "Do you really think AIR believes that?"

"No," Rider said. "However, I think outsiders might think so. Especially since Vincent is a Walker."

I never thought about the situation like that. "But he disappears on his own. It's what he does."

"Yes, but others may think we decided to rid ourselves of him," Rider said. "Most people fear Walkers."

"Maybe we should call and check in."

"You're both on medical leave," Taylor said. "Wait until Logan catches up, and then you can all compare notes. Now, Cassie, step in here, put on the robe, and knock on the door when you're ready."

I hated this part. Getting undressed at the doctor's office was awkward enough--when your doctor was also a friend, it was doubly weird. Taylor had always been good at putting me at my ease, but I didn't like it all the same.

Once I stripped down, Taylor led me into another room,

which housed the MRI machine. He glanced at Rider then pointedly looked at me.

"He can stay," I said. "Maybe you can help him, too. He wants the cast off."

"Didn't it go on yesterday?" Taylor asked.

"The day before," Rider said.

"I'll take new x-rays after this. Cassie, I want to test you normally first, then I'm going to ask you to use your abilities and I'll take some new readings."

"Why is the tube so small?" Rider asked.

"It needs to be this size in order to work best. There's a larger one in another room, but that's for Lost too large to fit inside this one."

Once ensconced inside, the machine banged and whirred around me in a discordant rhythm. While Taylor and Rider chatted in the other room, I squeezed my eyes shut. Normally I wouldn't say I'm claustrophobic, but stick me in a tube and shove my face so close to the top that my nose nearly touched and claustrophobia took on a new meaning for me.

I was fine...as long as I kept my eyes closed.

"Okay, Cassie, hold as still as possible and read the Path."

The words I dreaded. I took a meditative breath before making the jump.

Once again, the world behaved as it should for a few moments. The shimmering colors flowed in gentle rivers ready to be read.

Then it hit. Raw, naked power swept through me, boiling away all thoughts of reading my surroundings.

"Back off, Cassie," Taylor called out quickly.

My mind was slow to process his words.

I breathed rapidly and shook from head to toe. Then, I froze.

I sensed a figure standing at my feet.

I jerked my head up to catch sight and smacked it against the wall of the MRI.

"Drop it, Cassie," Taylor snapped.

I fled from the Path, fear driving the change. For once I didn't even care as the brilliant colors drained away.

"Get me out of here," I said, trying to keep my voice even.

Within seconds, I was sliding out of the MRI.

As soon as my head cleared the edges of the machine I shot up and looked around, half expecting to see someone else in the room aside from Taylor and Rider.

"Sit still." Taylor's voice held a bite, but when I looked at him, his eyes were wide and his face pale. "I need to check some things. Rider, please step out of the room. Cassie and I have to talk in private, got it?"

"Of course," Rider said, seeming a little hurt at the sting in Taylor's voice.

Taylor had a strange-looking pen light that he used to stare into my eyes, then he checked my heartbeat, blood pressure, and finally my reflexes.

"You know, I've only seen you this rattled once before," I said. "It wasn't good news for me then either. Talk to me."

"You first," Taylor said as he jotted down notes. "Tell me exactly what you saw and experienced."

I gave him a quick run-down, but stammered to a halt after I explained the pain.

"And?" Taylor asked.

"And what?"

"When you sat up you seemed confused and lost. I need to know everything."

"You know, you're starting to scare me."

"No stalling."

I sighed, then glanced at the door nervously. Rider wouldn't listen in on purpose, but what if he heard?

If I was going to tell anyone, though, it might as well be my doctor. "I wasn't alone in the room. While in the Path, I felt someone down by my feet."

"Have you experienced this before?"

I told him about the other instances.

"Now," I said after I explained. "What aren't you telling me?"

"Your brain lit up like dragon fire."

"I take it it's not supposed to do that?"

"Not like this. Honestly... I've never seen anything like it. If it's okay with you, I think I'll ask Neil to go over the results as well. I want to know if there are any patterns. In the meantime, don't use your abilities."

"You know I can't agree to that," I said. "You haven't even told me what you wanted us to help with. I may need to use my power."

"To be frank, I don't think you should be working on anything right now."

"You can't be serious. I'll go crazy if I'm not doing something."

Taylor sighed. "Get dressed and we'll talk. I'll be in my office."

I knew with a burning certainty that if I wasn't busy with something, I would spend my time worrying about Vincent. After I threw on my clothes I tracked down Taylor and Rider in Taylor's office.

"If I were to tell you to take it easy and not work," Taylor said when I came in, "what would you do?"

Rider grinned and appeared as though he tried hard not to laugh.

"I'd find a way to pitch in anyway, or I'd find something else to do," I said.

"That's what I was worried you'd say."

"I *need* to keep busy right now."

"Well, I'm not going to ask you not to help," Taylor said. "Mostly because you'd ignore me, but also because I think we need you. All of you. What I'm going to ask you to do, though, is refrain from using your abilities as much as you're able. And I'm giving Rider and Logan a list of things to watch out for while you're here."

"I'll do my best," I said. "It's not like I want to enter the Path right now." I didn't add that if pushed I'd use my power no matter what pain I might be faced with.

"That's good. The human mind isn't meant to do what your brain is doing. I'm not certain what the strain will do."

Was it the stress of my power that caused me to see things? The thought was worrying.

It was time for a change in subject. "So, what are we helping with?"

CHAPTER

THREE

"It might be good to have Logan join us before we go into details." Taylor grabbed a tablet and led us out of the room. "Let's go talk to Neil while we wait."

"It seems really quiet right now," I said as Taylor led us through the building.

"We're a little short-handed," Taylor said. "Gordon and Sable are out west. There's been talk about some disappearances so they pulled in a few people from other offices to join them."

"There are not any Lost staying here at this time," Rider said. "Last time you had several in residence."

"People come in off and on," Taylor said. "Much like the clinics at AIR, our visitors fluctuate."

Taylor rapped twice on Neil's door and stepped into the lab. You had to call the room a lab, because it couldn't be called an office. Neil did all sorts of work in the room, so it ended up looking like a cross between a rummage store and a college dorm. Strong incense filled the air, covering smells from the more mild forms of Neil's bad habits.

"Hey man," Neil said, looking up. He was hunched over some sort of equipment, but he had the glassy-eyed look of someone who was truly stoned.

"Hi," I said.

"I thought you were staying sober while we're under-staffed," Taylor complained.

"Shit, man, don't start," Neil said, setting up a metallic box on a tripod.

"Well, I need you to review some test results later and put that mind of yours to work."

"I have my own tests," Neil said. "Like, do you seriously believe I don't have shit I'm doing?"

"Regardless, this is for Cassie, and you're going to help the second you're sober," Taylor said. It seemed like he was having a hard time keeping a lid on his temper.

"Dude, you only had to say. What kind of tests?"

Taylor dropped a file folder on the table next to Neil. "Brain scans."

"Dude," Neil said, turning to me. "If there's, like, something wrong with your brain we'll find it."

I grinned, but felt my cheeks color.

Neil flipped through the paperwork, not seeming to focus on anything.

Taylor glanced at his watch. "We're meeting as soon as Logan can join us. I want you there."

"Sure, man," Neil said. "When..."

Neil distractedly trailed off as the door opened and a woman stepped in. She appeared to be younger than me, but older than Neil, putting her maybe in her mid-twenties. Her hair was long and dark, and she stood almost a head taller than me.

"Angel, let me introduce you to our guests. Cassie, Rider,"

Taylor gestured at each of us in turn. "This is Angel. I think she was on assignment the last time you stayed in the city."

"I've heard a lot about you," Angel said, shaking my hand. "And not nearly enough about you," she added to Rider with a grin playing across her lips. "So, you're AIR agents"

"Working for the man," Neil said.

"We all have to work somewhere," Angel said, without taking her eyes off Rider.

"I wanted to check in with Neil to find out if he had those sensors ready," Angel said.

"They're here, man." Neil turned to Rider. "Dude, you're like a werewolf or something, aren't you? That might come in handy."

A buzzer went off, which once again distracted Neil. He went to a screen and flipped it on.

"So," Angel said after a few moments of silence, "you're a werewolf. I'd love to hear more about that. Do you run with a local pack?"

"Wrong kind of werewolf," Neil muttered almost under his breath.

"There are packs here?" Rider shifted and stood straighter, suddenly looking more on guard.

"They aren't from your world," Taylor said. "They're closer to shifters than they are actual werewolves."

"I do not know what the difference is," Rider said. "I thought there were very few werewolves in this world."

Angel's cheeks turned pink.

"The people Angel is referring to will likely seem wrong to you," Taylor said. "They aren't from your world, so they won't have the right smell and there are distinct cultural differences."

"Have you, like, watched any movies about werewolves?" Neil asked.

"They are made up," Rider said.

"Yeah... but, like, they're closer to the werewolves we have than you are. Not, like, the horror stuff, but the rest of it."

"I have not run across any at AIR," Rider said.

"You likely won't," Taylor said. "They're from this world. AIR tends to lump people from this world into one category.

"Oh man," Neil interrupted, tapping on a screen. "Sampson is here and he looks pissed."

I found the information about werewolves fascinating, and I wanted to hear more, but finding out what Neil watched on his computer monitor vied for my attention.

Taylor eyed Neil's screen before heading to the door. "This isn't good."

"It looks like fun to me," Angel said, almost laughing. She beat Taylor to the door and rushed out first.

I glanced at Rider and was certain his puzzled look mirrored my own. Without saying anything, we followed the others.

Taylor moved swiftly through the halls while Angel practically skipped toward the front entrance.

"Who's Sampson?" I asked, jogging to catch up.

"One of the local Lost," Taylor said. "A minotaur. Most of the time he's fine, but when he's agitated he can be a handful."

A loud roar came from the front of the building, which made me slow down. Taylor and Angel on the other hand, sped up. The crashing sound followed by breaking glass sounded like more than just a 'handful.'

"He certainly does not sound happy," Rider said, trotting fast.

"Sable!" the roar reverberated down the hallway.

Angel disappeared around the corner and I put on a spurt of speed, imagining what a raging minotaur could do to a seemingly unarmed person.

"Sampson," Angel said, sounding as though she greeted an old friend. "It's good to see you."

Taylor reached the entrance with Rider and I close on his heels.

I skidded to a stop when the minotaur bellowed again.

"Sorry, Sampson," Taylor said. "Sable's out of the office."

"You!" Sampson hollered. "What are you doing about this?"

Angel approached, still with a smile playing across her face. "We're working on it, big guy."

"If you'd like to come back to the clinic, perhaps we can talk," Taylor suggested.

Sampson's eyes landed on Taylor and narrowed. He took a step toward the doctor.

"I don't think so, big man," Angel said, sliding in front of Taylor, blocking Sampson's way.

Sampson's fist came out of nowhere. I opened my mind and ripped into the Path, accepting all that came with my power. Beside me, Rider surged forward.

We were too late. The attack was too fast for us to help.

Angel put up her hand to intercept the blow--and stopped the minotaur's hand dead in the air.

Feeling less than useless as agony scorched my brain, I pushed the Path away. I was so relieved to let it go that I almost missed Sampson's second punch.

Angel fielded it as easily as the first.

Once the ghosted memory of pain faded, I watched, fascinated by the display. Rider, too, stopped, seemingly intrigued.

"Come on, Sampson," Angel said. "Let's go for a walk to Taylor's office.

The minotaur roared again. Sampson was well muscled and stood more than a foot taller than Angel, but she easily gripped one arm and twisted it behind his back. She noticed Rider watching and winked at him.

"Taylor, why don't you lead the way," Angel said.

Taylor gave us quick directions to the conference room, and then hurried off with the others. Rider and I watched them go, then took in the state of the front entrance. Glass littered the floor.

"That was... interesting," Rider said.

"It was unexpected, that's for sure," I said. "They'll probably be a while. Let's find a broom or something. There has to be a closet around here."

Once we found supplies we set to work cleaning the area until Logan arrived. He scrutinized the hole in the glass and whistled before stepping though.

"Looks like you've rustled up an outlaw," Logan said.

"Just a visitor. A minotaur named Sampson came in, and he was pretty upset," I said.

"I can tell. Did someone tranq him?"

"No," Rider said. "Angel intercepted him."

"Angel?" Logan said with a grin. "She's a whole ball of fun, but I haven't seen her in a real fight. I thought she was human."

"If she is, then she's got a little something on the side," I said. Thinking again about what I saw, I amended that statement. "A lot of something on the side."

"She is not human," Rider said. "I have never come across someone like her."

"Logan," Taylor said, joining us again, "it's good to see you." He gestured for us to put aside the brooms.

"Heard you had a spot of trouble here in the city," Logan said. "I'm happy to help. It'll be good to be away from the office for a spell."

"What happened to Sampson?" I asked, following Taylor and Logan.

"Angel's seeing him out now," Taylor said. "We've had a

few problems in town. Actually, Sampson lives in the country, and he was just hit. Our dilemma is growing."

"What kind of issue do you have?" Rider asked.

"Thefts," Taylor said. "But it's not normal everyday possessions being stolen."

"Expensive stuff?" Logan asked.

"Yes and no." Taylor opened a door and gestured us inside. "The items are all religious, or culturally significant to the type of Lost they're taken from. Do you have your tablets with you?"

"I've been in another world," I said. "I don't have anything but my phone."

"It's best we keep anything from the office turned off for the time being." Logan didn't seem intent on explaining himself.

"No problem," Taylor said. "I'll put the information up on the screen."

Taylor plugged in his computer, and we all faced to the end of the conference room as the nearly wall sized screen came to life.

Neil entered the room, looking less glassy eyed than before, but still doped-up. He slid a tablet to Logan.

Logan immediately passed it on to me. Having a computer was too much like handling paperwork for the elf.

"These are things we'd like to keep off of AIR records as much as we can," Taylor said.

Logan took off his cowboy hat and dropped it on the table. "No worries there. Right now, the less contact with the office the better."

"Why is there secrecy around this?" Rider asked.

Taylor pulled a picture up on his laptop. It looked like a drawing of a piece of wood. "This might explain it. First up, we have the druids."

Logan whistled, and I stared at him blankly, not understanding why he seemed surprised.

"I don't know anything about druids," I said.

"Me neither," Rider added.

Taylor's phone rang. He glanced at the screen before silencing the call.

"They're pretty rare," Logan said, eyeing Taylor.

"Not so much rare as underground," Taylor said.

"No, man," Neil interrupted. "Just unperceived. We don't actually know how many populate the city, much less the state, country, or world. They were, like, decimated by the Celts."

"I thought druids were Celtic?" I said.

"The druid religion and way of life were taken over and incorporated into the Celtic society," Neil said. "The race of druids, however, was almost wiped out. To survive, those that didn't run away joined the Celtic people. Although join makes it sound voluntary. The records aren't very clear if it was."

"It wasn't until the 20th century that they resurfaced, and even then it was done quietly," Taylor said.

"AIR wouldn't be too interested in them, since they're locals," Logan said. "But to be on the safe side, we'll be sure not to mention it in certain company."

"If we are talking about people, why are we focusing on a drawing of wood?" Rider asked, motioning at the screen.

"That's what was stolen," Taylor said.

I raised an eyebrow and watched Taylor, waiting for more.

"It's kind of like a religious item," Taylor said.

"If you ask me," Neil said, "it's a symbolic representation of man's effect on nature, but whatever."

Taylor shook his head. "Regardless what people think about the relic, it's actually the remains of their sacred tree."

Neil rolled his eyes as Angel joined us, wordlessly taking a seat.

"Is it valuable?" I asked.

"It's carbonized wood," Neil said. "To be honest, it's only worth anything to a druid. No one else would care about it."

"That makes it sound like we're looking for another druid," Logan said.

"That seemed like a possibility." Taylor clicked a button and brought up a new image. "But the next item that we know about was stolen from trolls. Due to the nature of the item, anyone could have a motive to steal it."

"Is it quartz?" I asked, inspecting the picture of a large, rough, and very shiny rock.

"It's an uncut diamond," Taylor said.

Logan whistled seemingly as impressed as I felt about a diamond the size of a basketball.

"Once again," Neil said, "they've stolen carbon."

"Is that important?" Logan asked.

Neil rubbed his head. "There's not enough data to provide a significant correlation between the incidents."

"How many thefts have you had?" I asked.

"Five so far," Taylor said.

Neil dropped his hands and glared at Taylor. "I thought there were four."

"Sampson let us know about the latest one."

"What were the third and fourth?" Rider asked.

Taylor put up another picture for us. "The third was from the local gnomes."

I sat up a little straighter, staring at the wooded landscape Taylor showed us. "Isn't that the gnome homestead where Am died?"

"It is," Taylor said.

"What could they steal from a gnome?" I asked.

"The homestead," Taylor said. "Part of it, anyway. You

know how gnomes feel about their home."

"Were any of them hurt?" Rider asked. "My friend Indi lives there."

Taylor cleared his throat. "No injuries were reported at that location, and no one saw who stole their land. It was just dug up one night."

"No injuries *there*," Logan said. "Meaning someone was hurt elsewhere?"

"There's a local shaman that surprised intruders," Taylor said. "He ended up with a broken arm and concussion. That's when I decided it was time to bring in more help."

"Could he describe his attacker?" Logan asked.

"There were two men," Taylor said. "Both human in appearance, but they wore masks. Ski masks, nothing out of the ordinary."

"Did they get what they were after?" I asked.

"They did." Taylor clicked a key on his computer and a new image appeared. "This small statue was stolen."

"Is there a better picture?" Rider asked. "This one is very blurry. I can't make it out."

"He doesn't like being photographed," Taylor said as he flipped to another picture, this one a drawing.

My eyebrows raised once again. "He?"

"He," Taylor confirmed. "The statue has a soul inside."

I couldn't help but turn to Neil.

"Yeah, man. Just like your turtle."

The turtle Neil had created for me also held a soul--or possibly the entire body of a person--inside, along with a void. Another Walker, formally Vincent's friend, tried to take my soul and found more than he could handle. He released a void that had been trapped inside me. The void swallowed Cole, but before anyone else was torn apart I managed to trap the void.

The little stone turtle lived in my sock drawer.

"I performed some of the same rituals and stuff that shamans used to create their vessels." Neil pointed at the screen. "This one holds the soul of another shaman."

The drawing held more detail than the photograph, but it was still hard to recognize. The oblong stone had lines carved into it, but they were worn nearly smooth by age.

"They say it was a great source of power for the tribe," Taylor said. "The Shaman gave up his soul in order to bring his people good fortune."

"What was the final item stolen?" Logan asked.

It was Angel that spoke. "It was a minotaur horn. Said to be from Asterion, the first known minotaur to come to this world. Sampson is pretty upset by it."

"Heard you had a tussle with Sampson," Logan said.

Angel smiled. "Sampson's okay when he's calm, but he's all sorts of fun when he gets riled up, too."

Logan caught Angel's grin.

"Why would anyone want these things?" Rider asked.

"It seems to me," Logan added, "that the items are only important to their respective races, except maybe the diamond. Has anyone asked for money or anything in exchange for returning the relic?"

"Nothing so far," Taylor said.

"It's not likely they'll ask for it now," Neil said. "Probability indicated they would have started asking for ransom days ago if that was their goal."

"So, chances are they want them for something else," Logan said. "Has anything else unusual happened?"

"Dude, the cats were strange if you ask me," Neil said.

Angel glowered, losing any good humor. "Something like that sounds like the work of humans."

"What about cats?" Rider asked.

"Three were found in one neighborhood," Taylor said. "All

of them drained of blood. I agree with Angel on that one, but it's something you could check into."

"There was a portal stutter a week ago," Neil said.

"What's a portal shutter?" I asked.

"Like, the portal opens, but not quite. It turns on and off again as though it's stuttering," Neil explained.

"Was that in the city?" I asked quickly. "What day?"

"It was in the country," Neil said. "I'm sure AIR has it recorded."

"I know they have at least one recorded recently," I said. Glancing at Taylor, I asked, "Does everyone know where I've been?"

"MyTH helped your team while you were gone," Taylor said. "This portal stutter happened a day before you made it home."

"It could be related to my return," I said.

"How so?" Taylor asked.

"Do you all know how I got back?" I asked.

"Just what you told me when I was at your house," Taylor said.

"Something from the other world open a portal," I said. "When it started to fall apart, I forced it to reopen. From our world it might have looked like a stutter, like you mentioned."

"I'm still not seeing the connection, since this occurred on a different day," Taylor said.

"The thing that tried to open the gateway to our world didn't originally come from the gremlin world," I said. "To help us get home, someone from this world led it to us."

"What was it?" Neil asked.

"A sordis. Well, it looked like one anyway, but it's a type of demon," I said.

"It could be related to your return," Taylor said. His phone rang again, and his frown became more pronounced. "If you'll excuse me for a minute, I need to take this." He left the room staring unhappily at his phone.

Logan turned his attention to me and Rider. "So, what do you reckon our next steps should be?"

"We could see if the cat case is related," Rider said. "It does sound like something that needs to be investigated."

"Let's do that tomorrow morning," Logan said. "Is there any sort of pattern to when or where the thefts take place?"

Taylor returned looking agitated.

"They either happen in the early hours of morning or at night," Neil said. "The amount of time between thefts is narrowing, though. I'll analyze the information Sampson gave us, and then I can see if the timeline is being restricted at a measured rate. I can also put together a map to review."

"Let's meet here first thing tomorrow," Logan said.

"That sounds like a good idea," Angel said. "Rider, do you want to grab dinner with me?"

I'm not sure why the question surprised me, but it did.

"I do not think we have anything else planned," Rider said. "I will need Taylor to check my arm first."

"I also need to bend Rider's ear for a few," Logan said. "Yours too, Cassie. After that, he's all yours."

"Will you be joining us?" Rider asked.

"I'm eating with Jonathan tonight," Logan said.

Rider looked at me expectantly.

Angel cocked her head, as though wondering what I might say.

"I think I'll pass." I grinned at Rider. "Thanks, though."

"I'll send him your way shortly," Logan said.

Angel took the hint and left, and Neil trailed behind. When Taylor tried to leave, Logan stopped him.

"Hold up, Doc," Logan said. "I'm afraid this is going to affect you as much as it does our team."

FOUR

Taylor sat back down. When his cell phone rang once more, he didn't even glance at the screen, choosing to silence it instead.

"Hank gave me a run down," Logan said. "Fellows from DC are coming in and they want to talk to me and Cassie. Kyrian isn't keen on the idea, so she's going to hold them off for now."

"This is all because Vincent disappeared, isn't it?" I asked.

"It's true--the sooner he gets back, the better," Logan said. "For now, though, Hank is rerouting government calls away from your phone."

"How does this affect Taylor?" I asked.

Logan gave a nod in Taylor's direction.

"Your office has contacted me several times. They want consent to contact you," Taylor said. "At the moment, you, Logan, and Rider are out on medical leave."

"How did you get medical leave?" I asked Logan, knowing the elf hadn't been injured.

"Kyrian put me in for a psych evaluation," Logan said, then smiled. "It's been a rough few weeks after all. I'm not sure how long she can hold them off, but for now, as long as Taylor okays the leave, we're set."

"Medical leave isn't going to work long for Rider, so I think we'll need to add the psych eval for him as well," Taylor said.

"Fair enough," Logan said. "I'm off to find Jonathan. Enjoy your date tonight, Rider."

"I'm going to catch up with Neil before he decides to get high again," Taylor said. "Rider, I'll meet you in the clinic. Cassie, do you want to bring Frank to the lab later?"

"Sure," I agreed, standing.

Rider was slow to rise, so I stuck around while the others left.

"What's up?" I asked.

"This is a date?" Rider asked. "I did not realize."

"Angel seems nice."

"I am not sure what to do."

I wished Vincent was available for the date talk. "Don't make a big deal out of it. Be yourself and let her take the lead if you're uncomfortable doing so."

"What do people discuss while on dates?"

"Small talk." That sounded like the worst advice I could give to my literal-minded friend, so I continued on hurriedly. "You just get to know each other. Not in depth or anything on a first date, but you two kind of try to find out if you like each other enough to go out on a second date."

"Right," Rider said, finally rising. "I can do that."

"How is dating done in your world?" I asked.

"It is not the same. We have a better understanding of the other person beforehand. You know already if the person likes you and vice-versa. Smell accounts for a lot."

"Do you know when a person likes you here?" I asked.

"It is noticeable most of the time. Which is why I do not understand you and Vincent."

"I'm not sure I understand us any better."

Rider patted my shoulder. "He will be back soon, and then you will sort it out."

"Do you know if Angel likes you already?"

"She is too different from anyone I have met to know for sure."

"Do you like her?"

Rider grinned. "I cannot tell that either."

"Fair enough. Just remember, don't talk about how she smells."

"I have learned to avoid the subject."

I chuckled. "Have fun tonight."

Rider headed in one direction to get his cast off and I went the other to pick up Frank. Knowing Taylor was busy, I took my time.

Less than an hour later, with my rabbit in hand, I searched for Taylor. I heard arguing before I reached the clinic and it wasn't a surprise to hear who the voices belonged to. Taylor and Neil regularly rubbed each other the wrong way. Taylor got upset when Neil fried his brain on drugs and Neil became agitated anytime he sobered up.

I knocked on the door, cutting off their argument.

"Come in," Taylor called.

When I entered the room the two looked as though nothing out of the ordinary happened, which might be true for the pair--arguing was probably a routine occurrence.

"How has Frank been doing?" Taylor asked.

I blinked at Taylor and then eyed my zombie rabbit. "I haven't been home long enough to know. Vincent took care of him while I was gone. Frank's still eating."

"I'm not certain," Taylor said, "but eating may actually be more habit than necessity. Go ahead and put him on the table."

"That rabbit is, like, crazy strange," Neil said. "That's the

40

trouble with magic--unless you know the methods, there doesn't seem to be any logic behind it."

"Does that mean there's logic involved in creating Frank, but we don't know what it is?" I asked, taking a step back when Taylor pulled Frank out of his cage.

"I know a few witches," Neil said. "They make the best drugs, but they never stay in business long enough and give up the practice pretty quickly. When they cast their spells, though, there seemed to be a logic behind the actions or at least a balance."

"Any amount of time spent making drugs is too long," Taylor said, sounding almost absentminded while examining Frank.

"Like you'd know," Neil snapped.

"Some day you might put your brain to work on finding a solution to regulating information and adapting to other people," Taylor said.

"Dude, I have," Neil said. "That's what the drugs are for!"

Taylor shook his head not looking up.

"If you'd write me some script I wouldn't need to go find my own," Neil said.

"Never going to happen," Taylor said.

Neil made an exasperated noise and started for the door.

"There's a file on my desk," Tyler said.

"Take your file and--"

"They're Cassie's records," Taylor said, interrupting him.

"Right," Neil said. He let out a sigh and wouldn't look at anyone as he snatched the file up and left the room.

I watched him go, and when I turned around Taylor was where he had been before, but Frank wasn't. Puzzled, I looked at his cage, which was empty, and then movement on the floor caught my attention.

"Is that good for him?" I asked, moving back.

"He's dead. I'm not sure anything is good for him anymore."

Frank hopped toward me. The little fur-ball was so cute that I didn't even back further away.

"I don't know what to do with him," I admitted.

"If you're okay with it, I'd like to keep him here at MyTH for a while," Taylor said. "There are a few things I want to try."

"He doesn't appear to be in pain or anything."

"I don't believe he can be," Taylor said.

"How is it that he can still eat?" I asked, wanting to explore all I could.

"He's frozen in a moment. Rabbits don't think about too many different things, his body is still working as though he were in that moment."

"But he is dead, right?" I asked.

"He's trapped at a specific point in time, but yes, his body died. The magic is holding him together."

"So, I don't need to worry about bits of him falling off?" I asked.

"No bits should fall off. If we can find someone that knows enough necromancy to put an end to the spell, then he'd move on."

Frank brushed against my leg and I started. My first instinct was to run away, but I felt so bad for the little guy I couldn't bring myself to step away from him.

"So if you stop the spell--or reverse it, or whatever--he dies?" I asked. "I mean, really dies. Permanently."

"Is that what you want?" Taylor asked.

"I don't want him to be hurt, but it feels cruel to keep him hopping," I said. "I'm not sure how Molly is going to take to him either?"

"Molly?"

"Gran's new pet. She's sort of like, a guard cat," I said.

"Well, Frank can stay here for now. I'd like to work with him for a while."

"Doing what?" I asked.

"I'd like to begin by putting a cast or brace on his broken leg. He has trouble getting around and I think that'd help."

The idea of Frank being more active made me nervous, but I was becoming attached to the little fluffer.

"I'll want to run some more tests before we let him wander around too much, so for now, we'll keep him in the cage most of the time."

"He seems to prefer it."

"Perhaps."

MORNING ARRIVED FAR TOO QUICKLY. I tossed and turned all night, wondering where Vincent might be, then I stumbled out of bed at what felt like an unseemly hour. Getting ready for the day was done halfheartedly and upon exiting my room, I ran straight into Logan.

"Howdy, partner," Logan said.

Oh god, he's chipper. "Mmmhmm," was the best answer I could give. I made my way to the communal kitchen where Logan thoughtfully had coffee ready.

"So, I hear the doc checked you out yesterday."

"Yeah," I poured coffee and ladled sugar into the cup. It was too hot when I drank it, but I wanted the caffeine. "Where's Rider?"

"Haven't seen him yet today."

Taylor came in, looking almost as tired as me. It was nice to see someone else who wasn't a morning person.

"Do we have a plan about where to start investigating the thefts?" I asked

"It depends on what Neil has for us," Logan said. "But I thought we'd start with Sampson and work our way back as needed. Between Rider's sense of smell and your reading, we should be able to find something."

"Um--"

Taylor appeared surprised. "He doesn't know?"

"There's been no time," I said.

"Is this about the headaches you've had since you came back?" Logan asked.

Taylor looked questioningly at me.

"It's okay to tell him," I said. "He needs to know, there's just been no time until now."

Taylor gave Logan a quick rundown of what had happened yesterday. I realized my mistake almost immediately. It was probably better for Logan to know about me seeing or sensing something else in the Path, but the truth was, I wanted to leave that out of the conversation.

"So, you're not alone in the Path?" Logan asked.

I shrugged and didn't say anything. Rider walked in, and I was grateful for the distraction. To hide my relief, I refilled my coffee.

Rider grabbed a cup as well, and when he neared I noticed his eyes were drooped and he stifled a yawn. Rider was usually as much of a morning person as Logan was.

"How was last night?" I asked Rider.

He didn't have a chance to answer before Neil poked his head into the room.

"We're set up in the conference room," Neil said.

I grabbed my coffee and followed the others.

"You find anything interesting?" Logan asked.

"Well," Neil said, looking cranky, "that depends on your definition of interesting."

Neil entered the meeting room, which was set up much like yesterday.

"Anything that will help with the case?" Logan asked, trying again.

"There isn't enough data to form a strong correlation between the inciting incidents, but using the information I created a basic forecast." Neil clicked a few buttons on his laptop. "I also considered conditions of the localized area."

"What kind of conditions?" Taylor asked.

"The basics," Neil said. "Time of day, crime rates, weather patterns, concentration of possible targets, order of events, traffic patterns--"

"Would those things affect where they go?" Logan asked. "They're looking for pretty specific items."

"Since we don't know who *they* are," Neil said, "we don't know what will affect their next choice of target."

"Do we have any idea of how many of those sort of artifacts are in the city?" I asked.

"These aren't things the supernatural community usually discuss outside their own people," Taylor said.

"An interesting pattern can be discerned from the activity which already occurred," Neil said, barreling forward. "Note the areas and the order in which the incidents occur."

"It looks pretty random," I said.

"No. Randomness is unpredictable," he said, rubbing his forehead. "There are some intelligible predictions we can make based on information gathered. People are almost never purely random. In this case, the criminals we're looking for are trying to make us perceive their activities as random. So the lack of what people think of as random shows the actual pattern."

Rider blinked at Neil as though trying to get the words to line up in a way that would make sense to him. "What does that mean?"

Neil stared at him blankly for a minute. "People don't understand what randomness is."

"I'm beginning to think I don't either," I admitted.

"Dumb it down for us, kid," Logan said.

"I thought I had," Neil said, sounding cross.

"Neil," Taylor warned.

Neil rubbed his head again. "They tried to make us think the targets were random, but the idiots created a pattern just by attempting to look unpredictable."

I could almost see Neil's mind whirring, as though he was trying to be careful of the words he chose.

"Here are locations that are more probable to both have an item they're looking for and fit the way they move."

He pulled up another map of the city, which had areas glowing in varying shade of reds, yellows, and blues.

"I'll be back in my lab." Neil left without another word.

I felt bad for him as we watched him go.

"You'd think with as many drugs as that kid does, that brain of his would be fried by now," Logan said.

"It is," Taylor said. "That's the troubling part."

"Well," Logan said, "at least we have a starting point."

"He left off the cats," Rider said."

Taylor got up and studied the map. "It's in one of the orange areas."

"The cats should be investigated," Rider said. "But I am still not sure why it would be related. The items stolen sound like they can be very powerful for the original owners."

"They can be," Taylor agreed. "But so is blood. I'll admit, with the way these guys are working, human blood would be more likely, but blood taken from a living creature has power. There are several races which could use that type of energy, but they don't like to draw attention to themselves. The supernatural community frowns on anything that outsiders might notice."

"I'm guessing witches can use it, but then, other magic users could as well," Logan said.

Other magic users? I filed the idea away to ask about later.

"So we should search for magic users?" Rider asked.

"It couldn't hurt," Taylor said. "We don't have a lot of witches in the city, but the younger crowd has started moving in."

"Moving in... out from under the supervision of the elders," Logan said. "There could be something to that."

"Is there a way to, I don't know, detect magic?" I asked.

"I'm sure it would stand out to you while you're Reading," Logan said.

"Any other way?" I asked, trying to avoid the idea of using my power.

"A witch could detect magic," Logan said. "A few other supernaturals can as well. Witches could also make something to locate it. Even if we knew someone willing to whip up a magic tracker, it could take a while to create.""

"Are any Lost good at finding magic?" I asked.

Logan sighed. "Officially, no." He regarded each of us in turn. "And officially, it'll stay no. Are we clear?"

I had no idea what he was talking about, but I trusted my partner, so I nodded in agreement.

"If it's magic--real magic, not a human ability--I might be able to spot it."

"You can see magic?" I asked.

"Not exactly," Logan replied. "And that's all I'll say on the matter."

The elf was always cagey about telling other people what he could do and I wasn't going to pry. Thankfully for me, he had always hid a lot of knowledge about my power from the agency. Now I knew better and censored my reports.

"So, what's our plan?" I asked.

"The cats," Rider said. "We can start from where the cats were found and see if there is magic involved."

My stomach twisted at the thought. "I hate the idea there's anyone that would do that to an animal."

"Well, if it's not a human doing it and its not related to our case, we may have even more trouble," Logan said. "I only know a few reasons to drain blood, and most of them involve food. Have any larger animals been found?"

"Nothing," Taylor said. "We've kept an eye on emergency calls across the city."

"Let's hope it stays that way," Logan said. "We'll see if the incident with the cats is part of our case, then go from there. Let's saddle up in an hour."

"I'll be in the clinic if you need me," Taylor said as he stood. "Keep this tablet with you while you're here. Neil swears it's safe. Your office won't be able to access it."

A HALF HOUR later I was over-caffeinated and ready to get out of the building. I spent about five minutes with Neil before he started getting cranky. Visiting Frank took up a little more time, and then I sat in my room for a while, worrying about Vincent. There had to be something I could do that wouldn't leave me time to dwell on him. I tried pacing the halls for a while, thinking about the investigation, but since we didn't know much, it wasn't distraction enough.

We took Logan's car, a four-door SUV which seemed tiny compared to our usual SWAT-style work truck.

"So, are we just going to walk around the area?" I asked.

"A little driving and a little walking," Logan said. "We'll nose around--literally, in Rider's case--and see if we find anything out of place. It's a week day so lots of people will be at work, but there will be some people around. We can ask if they've seen anything strange."

Canvassing an area didn't sound like it would be enough to keep my mind off Vincent, but I needed to make it work.

Once we arrived I noted that there were more people leaving the neighborhood than returning home. We went straight to the spot where the cats were reportedly found, and then we drove around for a while, circling out.

"The portal stutter Taylor and Neil mentioned yesterday, was it in this area?" Logan asked.

"The one that didn't quite open?" I asked. "It was miles from here. A lot further away from the city."

"I'd like to get a list of any Lost or supernatural person or animal in this area or close to the portal activity," Logan said.

"I'll text Taylor," I said.

It was a little after ten when Logan had finally had enough of driving.

"We'll start here," Logan said, taking us back to the address we started from. After he parked, we got out and scanned the street. "Why don't you all go one way and I'll go the other. Be on the lookout for injured animals and anything else out of the ordinary."

Rider and I walked quietly for a short time, but my curiosity got the better of me. "How did things go last night?"

"In what way do you mean?" Rider asked.

"Your date with Angel. Did you have fun?"

"It was... interesting."

"How so?"

"In her work she helps the Lost, but in different ways. And her job has fewer rules."

"Did you all spend all evening talking about work?"

"Most of the night. I know you suggested we get to know each other, but she seemed less inclined to discuss herself than I was. That left our jobs, and we talked about you, of course."

Inwardly I groaned "You talked about me?"

"You were gone for many days," Rider said. "Almost all my recent time was spent with the others, working to get you back."

"I didn't think of that. I guess it makes sense."

"I did not give details. I do not think the office would appreciate it, and I did not think you would either."

"You're probably right about AIR. Everyone is still trying to figure out exactly what happened and how."

"I feel as though we should be at the Farm helping them," Rider admitted.

"You might be okay going back--if you want to, that is. You weren't at my house when Vincent disappeared."

"I am concerned that they think you are responsible for his disappearance."

"People want to point a finger and nail down a reason for something as soon as they can. Boone was blamed for taking me to another world, remember? Hell, he was accused of killing me, while he was actually working to keep me alive."

"It sounds like you kept each other alive."

I shrugged. "We did the best we could, but were stuck in the wilderness. This is the type of wildlife I'm comfortable with." I waved my arm around the street. "Urban wildlife. The only camping I want to do needs to be equipped with a bed and a pillow. And there had better be a bathroom nearby as well."

Rider grinned, but it was weak. "I enjoy being outdoors."

"I don't mind going for a hike or something, but I'd rather avoid overnight trips for a while. Even with the hammocks keeping us off the ground, I don't think I'd enjoy it after being in the gremlin world."

"I am sorry you did not have us with you."

"Boone and I didn't get along right away, but it wasn't so bad after we understood each other a little better."

"I am very thankful for him."

"Me too. So, after talking with Angel," I said, changing the subject, "do you think you like your job more or hers?"

"I am not sure. The local offices are here, though, and I would not want to live in the city. And I would still want to work with you, Vincent, and Logan. We are a good team."

I grinned. "We are, aren't we."

Rider stopped, and I looked around to see what had caught his attention. He had his head cocked, so I waited, knowing he would fill me in on what he discovered as soon as he was ready.

"There is a smell," he said at last.

"What kind of smell?"

"Old blood."

My nose wrinkled involuntarily. "Human?"

"I do not think so." Rider began to wander down the street, eyeing the houses before pointing between two buildings. "It is that way."

"It looks like there's an alley behind the houses. Let's go around. I'd rather do that than risk someone being ticked off because we trampled their lawn." We went down the road and turned at the cross street. "So, do you like Angel?" I asked, trying to wheedle more information out of my friend. "I mean, you don't have to tell me if you don't want to, but..."

"I do like her. She is..." Rider grinned as though remembering something amusing. "She is different from the other men and women I have met in this world."

I smiled. "In a good way, I take it?"

"She does not have an issue with the clothes thing."

I blinked for a minute, working out what he was trying to say, then I tried to stifle a laugh. "Well, I'm glad you found someone who doesn't. Are you going to see her again?"

"She will be at the office later today. I do not know if we will be there at the same time or not."

I turned down the alley. "Not in that way. I mean, are you all going to go on another date?"

"I think so. We discussed--wait, slow down."

"What? Why?"

"We are approaching a large animal."

I slowed and studied our surroundings. "I don't see anything," I said, instinctively lowering my voice.

"It is ahead and to the right."

"It's probably a dog or something."

"It does not smell like a dog."

"What does it smell like?"

"Old blood."

A chill came out of nowhere and gooseflesh rose on my arms.

"Logan is on his way," Rider said.

"It could still just be a dog," I said, trying to convince myself.

"I do not think this is the case."

As we neared, a snarl issued from behind a tall wooden fence.

"There is an animal over there," Rider said.

"I can hear--"

"No. A cat. Up ahead."

I searched for movement, but instead I saw fur. Unmoving fur tinged with red.

I covered my mouth with my hand and approached. "It's a cat. It looks... dry."

"Logan asked if the animal is drained of blood."

"How can I tell? It definitely lost blood, but I don't know if there's still some left."

Rider joined me, and then something slammed against the fence beside us. A deep growl followed and fence posts shook as the creature tried to reach us.

"Logan says we should move away."

"You won't hear me arguing." I began to take a step back, and the beast became enraged. Wood splintered, but somehow kept together. I held my breath, waiting for the thing to assault the boards again. Instead, I heard the animal bound off.

I steadied myself and sighed with relief. "It was probably just upset we were close to its home. Come on, we can wait for Logan out on the main street." Rider turned to go, but I took a moment to inspect the dead animal, feeling bad for the poor thing.

Feet pounded on the ground behind the fence--the creature was running forward. Fearing it would break through this time, I jerked around.

My heart thudded hard in my chest as my mind worked fast to process what I saw. Sailing through the air was a horrendous sight. The *shape* was similar to a dog, but that's where the likeness ended. It was enormous. Matted tufts of fur on the body were spaced between large swatches of bare skin the color of wet clay. Each of the four legs had feet, but the claws attached were long and thin. Teeth protruded from its muzzle every which way, as though the mouth was so crowded some were trying to escape.

The hideous beast soared straight at Rider.

CHAPTER
FIVE

"No!" I screamed, for all the good it would do. Without hesitation, I jumped into the Path. A few moments of clear reading was quickly followed by the feel of my brain splitting into two.

It didn't matter, though. I grabbed hold of the Path between Rider and the creature and solidified the air. Rider crouched down, ready to pounce on his attacker.

My head felt like it was being pierced with hot needles. Each nerve ending erupted again and again.

The animal struck my shield and fell to the ground short of Rider. It jumped up, shook itself and slammed into the barrier again.

Clutching my head, I sunk down. Tears ran unchecked down my face, but I ignored them

I'm not sure if the creature saw my movement or sensed it, but the dog-like animal changed direction.

Rider snarled. The beast snapped its attention back to Rider, but only as it passed him while bearing down on me.

"Drop it, Cassie!" Rider barked.

The words were an order, plain and direct. As though on autopilot, I let go of my barrier.

The creature's feet pounded against the ground, talons clicking on the surface with each stride.

Then Rider was on the monster.

I kept reading, ready to use my power in any way I could. Yells came from behind me, but I couldn't make out the words over the racket Rider made. The pounding in my brain certainly didn't help.

After a few moments, the animal stopped struggling. Rider rolled off it, but crouched down low, prepared to pounce once again.

A hand fell on my shoulder and I jerked away before realizing it was Logan. I didn't wait for the suggestion to stop reading. I did so, gratefully, then pulled my knees to my chest and hid my eyes from the light. The sun wanted to slice its way through the holes in my mind left by the scorching Path.

"It should be out for a while," Logan said. "What kind of damned fool would keep one of these in their yard?"

"What is it?" I asked, lifting my head.

"A chupacabra. They're dangerous."

"Ralphy," a voice called out.

I stared at the creature, not believing what I heard. Ralphy?

"Here, boy. Here, Ralphy." A section of the fence rattled and gate swung open. An elderly woman with coke-bottle glasses stepped into the alley. "Hey now, what are you doing to my dog?"

My jaw dropped.

"I'm sorry, ma'am," Logan said. "This creature is yours?"

"He is. That's my Ralphy. What did you do to him?" The old woman's voice cracked at the end.

"He's okay," Logan said. "We just put him to sleep before

he could hurt anyone. Has this creature... I mean Ralphy. Has Ralphy ever attacked you?"

"Of course not," the old woman snapped.

"How long have you had him?" Logan asked.

"I found him about a week ago," the woman said. "He's a darling little lamb."

I looked at the hideous creature once again. Rider sat close to Ralphy, still ready to subdue him.

"I see," Logan said. "Do you mind if you and I have a word in private about Ralphy?"

"If you've hurt him, young man, there *will* be heck to pay."

"I assure you, he won't be harmed in any way," Logan said.

"I can't just leave him out here."

"My friends will look after him."

"Well, okay," the woman grumbled, returning to her yard.

Logan turned to us and said something in a low voice. I couldn't make out the words, but I was certain Rider could. Then Logan followed the old woman.

Rider waited until the pair were out of sight before standing and pulling out his phone to make a call. "Taylor, this is Rider. We need to export a creature and put him into containment."

"He is larger than a dog, but not by much," Rider said before giving Taylor the cross street and directions to our location. After he hung up, he walked over to me and sat down, all while keeping an eye on the chupacabra.

"Are you okay?" I asked. "I couldn't see if Ralphy got hold of you."

"There are some sort of spines on his back," Rider said, plucking at his t-shirt.

I inspected my partner, and sure enough, holes marred his shirt and pants. "How bad are the cuts?" I asked, leaning over to check for blood.

"I will heal soon."

I nodded and sunk back to the ground again. We rested quietly for a short time. "What is Logan telling the woman?"

"He is explaining Ralphy has another home where he is very happy and greatly missed."

"How is it that Ralphy didn't attack her?"

"She told Logan that the animal had been hit by a car. She wrapped him in a blanket and started to take him to the vet, but he recovered, so she took him home instead."

"It looks like he would maul anything on sight."

"Animals do not always attack those that have done them a kindness."

"True."

We sat in comfortable silence again.

"Taylor will be here shortly," Rider said after a while.

I only nodded.

"Are you able to stand?"

"Yeah," I assured him. "I'm okay."

To prove it, I carefully got to my feet. As my head swam, though, I worried I might fall back down.

"Logan would like for you to go back with Taylor," Rider said.

I mentally kicked myself for not getting up right away. Then I wanted to berate myself for falling down in the first place.

"I'm not hurt," I said without too much hope that either of my partners believing me. Rider sounded like he agreed with Logan.

"I know you are not, but I think it would be appropriate to ask Taylor to give you a checkup, just in case."

I didn't want to admit it, but my partners were right.

"We will join you at MyTH as soon as we have finished in the area."

That made me feel a little better at least. "Sounds good."

A large moving van turned slowly down the ally, and as it neared I saw Taylor at the wheel.

When he got close, he jumped out and came to look at what we found. We told him briefly what happened, not filling in any details beyond the animal attacking us and Logan tranquilizing the beast.

"A chupacabra has never been seen this far north," Taylor said. "I wonder how he got here."

"Where do they usually live?" I asked.

"Central America mostly, although they migrate as far as Mexico. I've never heard of one in the United States."

"Do you think there are more of them?" Rider asked.

"I'll reach out to the MyTH offices in Texas to keep an eye out for them, and I'll give the other offices a heads up. Let's get him contained before he wakes up."

Rider did the heavy lifting and Taylor examined the creature long enough to take its vitals before closing up the van.

"We'll keep him at MyTH for now," Taylor said.

"I'm going back with you," I said.

"Sure thing," he said without hesitation.

It wasn't until we were on the way back to the office that he asked the question, although it came out more of a statement. "You used your power when the chupacabra attacked, didn't you."

"I did."

"Give me the details."

I started out brief, but like a good doctor, Taylor pulled out the details, having me explain sensations thoroughly.

"We'll do a physical when we get back. Full blood panels, the works."

"I don't think this is something you're going to find in my blood."

"You're right," he admitted. "But until we figure out what the issue is, we'll keep testing."

"Have you or Neil discovered any hint of what's happening?"

"Not a thing. The kid is beating himself up over it. The experience is good for him, though. It's been months since I've seen him drug free for this long. I think since the last time you stayed, actually."

We drove around the back of the MyTH offices to the one small loading dock, which Taylor backed up to. I was surprised, however, that we left the chupacabra in the van and went inside instead.

"I don't think it's safe for him to stay in the truck for long," I said. "It's not hot outside, but it's still pretty warm."

"Angel is in the office. I'm going to ask her to bring the chupacabra in."

"Does she need any help?"

"Not likely. I'll call her on our way to the clinic."

He called, but I didn't pay too much attention to what he said as we wound through the building. Before we reached our destination Taylor stopped me. He held up a finger while wrapping up his conversation with Angel. Since I wasn't looking forward to yet another exam, I settled back against a wall, wanting Taylor to know I wasn't in a hurry.

When he hung up the phone, he looked uncertain.

"What's up?" I asked.

"I have another patient," Taylor said.

"Don't worry," I said. "I have no problem waiting."

Taylor gave me a knowing smile. "I'm sure you don't. How would you feel about Frank meeting some new people?"

"Is that safe?"

"Frank will be fine."

Frank getting hurt wasn't high on my list of concerns. As a

zombie bunny I was more worried about how Frank could affect others.

"There are two boys," Taylor said. "They've been having a hard time lately. While I talk with their mom, I hoped you would introduce them to Frank. I think it might be good for kids to be around an animal they can't kill."

That doesn't sound ominous at all. "Can't kill? Why would they kill him?"

"They wouldn't on purpose of course. Ana and her children are banshees, and young people don't always maintain the best control. They can't keep a pet at their age in case one of them screams. Actually, most adult banshees won't risk keeping an animal close, just in case."

"I don't know much about banshees," I admitted. "Could their power hurt Frank?"

"I'm not sure much of anything could hurt your rabbit. If he were alive, the scream would easily kill him, but now, Frank should be fine."

We heard someone talking down the hall.

Taylor lowered his voice. "Do you mind?"

"I guess it's okay," I said, not at all sure. "If it'll help and he'll be okay."

"Go ahead and let Frank out and see if they want to play with him."

"If you're sure."

A woman rounded the corner with a stressed out smile plastered on her face. She led two sulking boys by hand.

"Ana," Taylor said, turning to the woman. "It's good to see you."

"I was hoping I would catch you in the office," Ana said. "Do you have a few minutes?"

"Of course," Taylor said. "Ana, this is Cassie Heidrich. She's working with us for a short time. Would it be alright if she takes Mark and Watson downstairs while we talk?"

"If you think it would be okay," Ana said. "Mark, Watson, you two behave yourself."

Taylor disappeared and came back with Frank.

I had no idea how to get into the lower levels of Myth, which thankfully, Taylor realized quickly, and opened a door to a stairwell. He held the door open while the kids and I started downstairs.

The boys didn't say anything as we slowly made our way down. Since I wasn't sure where I was going, I stalled as much as possible. When we stopped at the landing to the basement I noticed the kids kept an eye on the rabbit.

"This is Frank," I said, holding up the cage for them to see.

They wordlessly stared at the animal, but didn't move closer. I was relieved to hear Taylor and Ana enter the stairwell.

"Right this way," Taylor said, whisking past us.

Ana grabbed her kids hands while Frank and I followed behind. Taylor opened a door and ushered us in.

"Cassie, go ahead and set Frank's cage in the middle of the floor and open it up for him," Taylor said.

I eyed him nervously, but went ahead and did what he asked.

"We can't keep pets," the older of the kids said. "We shouldn't have animals around us."

"Don't worry," I said, wishing I wasn't so anxious about the situation. "Frank is special."

"Use the room for as long as you need," Taylor said to Ana. "Just let us know if you need anything."

"No one will be around the room, right?" Ana asked.

"No one will bother you here. If you keep the door shut, no one will hear anything," Taylor said.

Ana nodded. I could tell she was almost as uncertain about Frank as I was, but she didn't say anything.

I gave Frank's cage a little pat and left the room. Taylor secured the door and I followed him upstairs.

"You're sure Frank will be okay in there, right?" I asked as we entered his office.

"I told Ana we'd keep an eye on him for the first few minutes," Taylor said, logging into his laptop. "But nothing should happen to Frank and I'm sure the kids will appreciate him."

Once Taylor pulled up the video of the room, I could tell Ana was being tentative. She watched the rabbit closely. She appeared to be yelling, but trying hard not to. Then I saw her let lose. There was nothing for us to hear upstairs of course, we only had the video, but Ana threw back her head and screamed. Static covered the monitor twice before the picture came back.

In the windowless soundproof room, Ana's hair spread around her as though it were trapped in a wild wind. Her appearance changed as well. She was gaunt and much older than she had been before.

Frank appeared to be fine. In fact, he munched down on another piece of lettuce. Ana stopped screaming long enough to say something to her kids, then all three opened their mouths.

The screen filled with static and the picture didn't come back.

"Frank didn't seem to be bothered by the sound at all," I said.

Taylor clicked a few buttons before giving up and closing the window on his computer. "It makes a strange sort of sense."

"Won't it hurt his ear drums or something?" I asked.

"I shouldn't think so. His body is stuck in one moment. Aside from the damage done to him at the time of his death, I don't think anything is going to injure Frank unless someone gets physically aggressive with him."

"I can't imagine anyone doing that. I mean, I'm not sure Gran's new pet likes Frank, but she's been introduced and knows he belongs in the house, so I don't think she'd attack him."

"There might be trouble if anyone from AIR found out about him," Taylor said.

"It's a good thing you're keeping him for a while, then. I'm worried about these people from Washington coming into the house."

"While he's here, if you're okay with it, I'd like to invite Ana and her kids to come and visit Frank."

"I think Frank would love someone to play with."

"He's the perfect pet for young people in similar circumstances," Taylor said. "Not just for banshees, but many kids in the area would love to play with an animal where they normally wouldn't be able."

"That sounds really nice for Frank," I said, already feeling as though I was losing the little fluffer.

"You can take him home whenever you want," Taylor reminded me. He must have heard something in my voice gave him an idea of what was on my mind.

"Frank is going to be happy here."

⁂

AN HOUR later I found myself in the lab with Frank, while we waited for Taylor. I couldn't help but let the bunny out and let him hop around.

"So," Taylor said when he entered, "Let's break your problem down."

Straight to business. I had been hoping we could ignore my 'problem,' but I knew it wasn't a real option.

"Where do we start?" I asked.

"What's different?" Taylor asked. "I mean, a few days ago you could work the Path okay, but now it's crippling."

"I'm not sure where to start."

"Go back to as early as you need to."

I thought back to when things started to go wrong. "You know how gremlins fix things?"

"You mean altering things, but not the way you'd want them to."

"Exactly. They wanted to do something nice for me, so they gave me some sort of liquid which mended my soul back together."

"That's... that's amazing."

"Except, like you said, they never repair anything the way you want them to. The change brought my power down to almost nothing. I couldn't even read a Path more than an hour or so old."

"And that's not so good."

"Not to me."

"Is that when your headaches started?"

"Yeah, but I thought holding the portal open caused those. I mean, I burnt myself out. Once I recovered, I was sort of making my power work for me again, even when my head hurt."

"Until?"

"Until the changeling attacked us at my house. There was nothing else we could do. The healing process on my soul wasn't complete, so, with Vincent's unintentional help, I broke my soul again."

"Define 'unintentional.'"

"He gave me a little boost of strength. I used the energy to break my soul again, so I'd have enough power to control the Path, not just read it."

"What happened?"

"It all went wrong. My head ached and my power was unwieldy. Since I couldn't do anything, Vincent took the changeling between the worlds."

Taylor jotted down a few notes. "And you?"

"It was painful, but not as bad as now. During that incident I first sensed someone else in the Path--aside from Fenrir, of course."

"And he is?"

"I'm not sure he'd like it if I talked about him." Then I remembered his loneliness. "Actually, he probably wouldn't mind. He's a person that looks like a wolf. He lives in the Path and can jump in and out of our world as much as he wants. At least it seems that way."

"Interesting," Taylor said. "And this time, you broke your soul yourself."

"Rider said I changed. He didn't think people and animals would be so aggressive towards me anymore, but he didn't say why."

"This may sound like an odd question, but does your soul feel any different?"

"I don't know," I admitted. "I never thought much about it."

"Give it some thought now, and while you do, I'm going to run some more tests. You may be wrong about this not showing up in your blood."

"What makes you think that?"

"The concoction the gremlins gave you mended your soul. It could still be in your system, trying to work, but by now it might be weak to the point it couldn't pull your soul together, yet still strong enough to do some harm."

"I'm all for finding out if that's the issue. If it is the gremlin medicine, is there a way to fix it?"

"We may just have to let it run its course, but if what they gave you is affecting you now, the effects should dissipate with time."

It was the first hopeful news I'd heard since Vincent disappeared, so I took it and held on tight.

Taylor drew blood, and afterwards I let him know I'd be back in my room, meditating. With Vincent gone I used up all my mental capacity worrying about him. After he left I hadn't thought about looking at the state of my soul. It was past time to find out what I had done to myself.

Before I met Vincent, I had never given any thought to souls, or the essence that makes me, me. The idea wasn't something I disbelieved--it was more that I had never considered the subject long enough to decide one way or the other.

Then, as an agency-sanctioned assassin, Vincent tried to kill me by taking my soul. Before he completed the task he realized his mistake, recognizing I wasn't the demon he had been told I was. To save my life, he did what he hadn't thought possible; he put my essence back into my body.

Unfortunately, as a result, my soul shattered into countless pieces. The effects turned out well for me. The shards amplified my power to unknown levels. More importantly to me, I ended up sharing a grain of my essence with Vincent and I had a small piece of him inside me. He knew me more deeply than I could fathom, even now. We understood each other in ways I never imagined.

When the gremlins fixed my soul all those fragments melded together, creating a rippling ocean of my essence. When danger came calling, I ripped myself apart once again.

Then, In trademark fashion, I ignored the problem as long as possible.

There was no choice but to face the facts and survey the mangled remains.

Once I settled in my room reaching my soul came easily. It was similar to reading. I'd mentally stretch and come to the edges of my knowledge, leaving all other thoughts and ideas behind me. If I'd been reading I would make the jump into the Path from that spot. Instead, I stopped.

A few days earlier there had been a calm flow in the darkness between my mind and the Path. After the internal damage I'd caused there was a brilliantly lit mess. Chunks of my essence churned, rubbing against smaller pieces and smashing into larger ones.

What have I done?

CHAPTER

SIX

When my soul had first been torn apart, the pieces had been sharp and glided smoothly between each other. Lucky for me, those shards reflected my ability, amplifying it.

The second breaking of my soul left a mess of fun-house curves. Power bounced everywhere, but it wasn't just amplified. When energy touched a piece of my essence it left twisted.

My mind stilled, stunned at the chaos. It was no wonder reading hurt—mentally I jumped through a disaster area. If this bedlam could be seen in the real world, where normal people could see, I would be quarantined--labeled too dangerous to work with.

I began to ease back, not wanting to witness anymore. At the same time, though, I had trouble looking away. As I mentally retreated something else caught my eye. A substance clung to part of my soul and it kept some of the pieces stuck together. When a contaminated shard pulled away or attempted to slide by another, the fragment sprung back, causing turmoil in its wake.

New thoughts tried to drag me back from the edge, but I pushed them away.

Could this be what the gremlins used to fix me?

My eyes fluttered open and tears flowed. I numbly laid back on the bed, staring at the ceiling. Where do you start reconstructing something so thoroughly destroyed?

Is it fixable?

Was I so far broken I wasn't worth the effort?

The latter felt like the real question, but I forced the thought away. I wasn't even sure this really affected me in any way aside from using my power. Being a Reader was part of who I was. But, it wasn't everything. Was it?

I built my life around my abilities, though, which meant disaster if I continued as broken as I was.

Although most of me still reeled in shock over what I found, a small part of myself was glad to have an idea of what was happening. There was also a tiny sliver that wanted me to go stick my head in the sand and ignore the whole thing.

This was too big to avoid. What if the next time something attacked, I couldn't fight through the pain to help?

Someone knocked at the door and without thinking, I said, "Come in."

Realizing my mistake, I shot up on my bed and hastily wiped away the tears from my face. I was relieved to find Rider entered alone.

"How's the case going?" I asked quickly.

"We brought the old woman a new dog which needed a home. Logan said it was a brother to Ralphy, and she appeared to accept the lie." Rider sat on the only chair in the room. "Did things go badly here?"

"No. And then again, yes."

"I do not understand."

"Me neither," I admitted.

"We have time before we leave. Do you want to talk?"

"Maybe." Did I?

He waited expectantly. Finally, I blew out a breath and told him what I found.

Getting the discovery into the open lifted my melancholy mood and I felt less alone with the problem.

"Do you think the gremlin medicine is trying to hold the pieces together?" Rider asked.

"Taylor brought up the idea--I never would have thought about it on my own. Now, though, I think it's a possibility."

"Do you have any ideas what to do next?"

"I'm not sure. The effects have to wear off sometime, right?"

Rider shrugged. "This is far beyond my understanding of how people work."

"Yeah, mine too."

"At least you know what you can do while you work out your next move."

"What's that?"

"Vincent suggested it the first time. Meditation. It might be possible for you to align yourself."

"I wish Vincent was here to help. I always did so much better meditating when we worked together."

"I will join you."

"I didn't know you meditated."

"I do not usually, but we should do this with each other."

"Sure." It was somewhat of a relief that I wouldn't be alone. "When do you want to start?"

"We have time before we gain access to the crime scene at the shaman's house. We can begin now."

MEDITATION WAS the usual frustrating process I always experienced when I fell out of practice. I was happy to call an end to it early, thankfully giving us enough time to grab lunch before meeting Logan at his car.

"How are things going this afternoon?" Logan asked as he drove to the edge of the city.

"I'm doing okay, but the problem is still there. I'm hoping meditation will help."

"I thought meditation was supposed to be less... squirmy," Rider said.

Logan snickered. He knew me too well.

"It's hard to get back into the swing of things," I muttered not quite under my breath.

"It will be easier for both of us once Vincent returns," Rider said.

He wasn't wrong. My mind flew to Vincent often. "What's the plan when we get to the crime scene?" I asked, trying to change the subject.

"We'll see if the shaman can give us anything," Logan said. "Now that we can rule out the feline incident, I'd like to concentrate on possible witnesses."

"Any theories on why someone would steal this stuff?" I asked. "All I've got is, it's weird."

"We can't discount anything yet," Logan said.

"Do we have any ideas to start with?" I asked

"Someone could be stealing them to sell off to the highest bidder," Logan suggested.

"Wouldn't the race it was stolen from pay the most?" I asked. "They're the ones it would mean the most to."

"I think they would ransom the objects if that were the case," Rider said. "Taylor indicated that no one has asked for money."

"As far as he knows. It's possible MyTH hasn't been told," I said.

"That is true," Rider said. "But the Lost are reporting the items missing. Would they not report the contact if they had the option of getting their artifact back?"

"At this point someone would have spilled the beans, even if they were told to keep quiet," Logan said. "With this many thefts, there would be no way to keep it quiet."

"The thieves could be waiting to ask for a ransom," I said. "Maybe their plan is to steal everything first, then reach out to everyone at once."

"Why would they wait?" Rider asked.

"I'm not sure. Are the artifacts particularly powerful at certain times?" I asked. "Like for ceremonies or something?"

"We can check on it, but I don't think that would apply to all of them," Logan said. "Using a random piece of a gnome homestead wouldn't be time sensitive, and it's not the only one."

"There's always the black-market," I said. The theory of rituals stirred another idea, but the theory needed time to form.

"If they have a buyer, they'd be rich," Logan said. "There's lots of people that would get a warm feeling inside just knowing they held that kind of power, even if they couldn't use or display the stolen items."

"Whoever possessed the artifacts would hold considerable influence over the other the previous owners," Rider said.

"That's a good possibility," Logan said.

"To what end?" I asked.

Logan shrugged. "Hard to say. City politics can be tricky, but I can't imagine anyone needing to exert that much control over these particular races."

"Could someone be threatening to expose the Lost?" Rider asked.

"Nah," Logan said. "Too many of these people are locals. AIR isn't interested in them, for the most part. Other organizations might be paying attention, but the artifacts aren't exactly evidence of anything, so exposure is probably not what we're looking at."

Logan parked in front of a house that looked very much like all the other houses on the street.

"So, power of one sort or another could be the motive," I said. "I wonder if all the victims share a specific enemy."

"Let's go find out," Logan said, getting out of the car.

We silently trooped up the sidewalk and Logan knocked on the door. A harried-looking woman answered with a scowl. Interestingly, her face softened somewhat when she saw Rider,

"Howdy," Logan said as he took off his hat.

She crossed her arms and waited for more.

"I'm Logan, and this here is Cassie and Rider. We're working with MyTH and understand you had a spot of trouble. We're hoping to ask a few questions. May we come in?"

The woman stepped aside and waved us inside. "What is MyTH doing about this?"

"We're investigating the theft in order to track down the party responsible and get your property back," Logan said. "I didn't catch your name."

"Annie," the woman said.

"Nice to meet you, Annie," Logan said. "Were you the person attacked?"

"No. Art is upstairs resting."

"Can you walk us through what happened?" Logan asked.

Without any enthusiasm, Annie showed us through the kitchen to the back door. "They broke in here and went into the living room." As she led the way she pointed out items that had been moved or jostled in any way. I took note of fingerprint dust on a few of the flat surfaces. Our tour ended at a door under the stairs. "We stored the statue in here."

It surprised me to hear that they kept such an important item in a regular closet.

"There's an alarm," Annie said. "When they broke into the room, Art was alerted and tried to stop the intruders."

"What kind of alarm?" Logan asked.

She opened the door and a loud screech pierced the air. Rider winced and she closed the door again.

"It's a simple device," Annie said.

"Is the artifact always kept in this room?" I asked.

The woman looked at me, surprised. "The statue has only been in the city for two days. If they had waited a week, it wouldn't have been here and the thieving bastards wouldn't have gotten their hands on it."

"Why was it here?" I asked.

"The relic rarely changes hands," Annie said. "But as the world evolves, the safety of our treasure is brought into question and a new, safer location is found for it to reside. This was just a short stop before Art, its caretaker, continued to the new home."

Rider began to roam through the rooms, taking in everything, while Logan chatted with the woman. I listened, but studied the room as well. The desire to reach for the Path was an itch that needed scratching, but I didn't want to risk it here—not in front of witnesses. Still, the whole situation didn't make much sense. If I wanted to find something that important, I wouldn't have thought to search below the stairs.

Through Logan's questioning I learned that the thieves took an almost direct route, straight to the object they came for. At least that's what it looked like since nothing else had been touched. Logan pressed Annie for the chance to talk to Art, but in the end, she only allowed Rider to go.

With Rider upstairs, Annie filled us in on the description of the intruders that Art had given the police and MyTH. One black and the other white. One slim and one heavy in build.

Logan's phone rang, interrupting his next question. The elf looked at the caller ID and excused himself. He was still close enough for me to hear.

"Howdy," Logan said.

After a few moments he said, "I see."

"Now," he said.

Hearing only his side of the conversation annoyed me, especially when Logan shifted from one foot to another, looking ready to run.

"You got it," Logan said, and hung up. "Cassie, let's wrangle Rider and get on out of here."

Before the words left his mouth, Rider ran down the stairs.

"Sorry to rush out," Logan called to Annie as he hurried me out the door. "We'll follow up later."

Logan and Rider almost ran to the car. I caught their urgency, and picked up my pace.

"What happened?" I asked.

"Taylor found us a fresh robbery" Logan said. "We'll need our badges on this one. Locals are on location."

I shifted in my seat. Back home, we knew someone on the police force and I didn't worry about working with them. I couldn't help but remember that it hadn't been easy at first, though.

Logan seemed to read my mind. "Taylor sent us the name of someone on scene who will be on the lookout for us."

"Good," I said.

"We're not sure this is one of ours, so we should stay in the background as much as possible," Logan said. "We're working with MyTH on this, not the police, and not AIR. We should find out what happened, but not involve ourselves to any further extent."

"If this is a Lost artifact, it should be related. What was stolen?" I asked.

Logan didn't answer right away and seemed reluctant to answer, but finally said, "A thorn from the Crown of Thorns was stolen."

A 'thorn' rang a distant bell, but I wasn't sure why.

"Why is a thorn important?" Rider asked.

"It's an artifact from the Catholic Church," Logan said. "They send the relics on tour throughout the world so that worshipers can see them. The crown of thorns was worn by the son of God when he died."

"Both human and Lost items being taken," I said. "What would be the point of that?"

CHAPTER

SEVEN

"If we're dealing with the black market, then there's a good chance the objects would sell to a wide variety of collectors," Logan said. "They'd be different markets since people who might pay top dollar for a human relic probably wouldn't be interested in something from a race which isn't supposed to exist."

"You're right," I said. "I can see zealots paying a high price for an artifact from the Catholic Church, but the same buyers likely wouldn't care about the rest."

"Knowing humans, having the other relics might even drive the offers down on everything," Logan said.

"Maybe." My mind churned with possibilities, all of them seeming possible, but no explanation fit the case perfectly. Except power.

"We need to split up as soon as we find Taylor's contact," Logan said. "Rider and I will track where they went when they left and hopefully follow who did this. Cassie, you stay on site and find out everything you can about our suspects and what they did."

The idea of being on my own made pixie's dance in my stomach, but I kept quiet. We pulled to a stop a block away from the yellow tape. After we took in the manic environment--emergency services, a news van and some gawkers were all getting settled in--we got out and wove our way through the vehicles which littered the road.

The officer Taylor mentioned waited for us at the edge of the chaos where we flashed our badges and were allowed behind the barricade. Once we were in, we parted ways.

I received a few looks and a nod as I walked up the stairs with Taylor's friend. In the building, though, he disappeared into the throng of emergency workers. When people broke apart to let a gurney through, I took note of the injured man before I squeezed by and went in search for the crime scene.

Once I passed the pews and went through a door off to the side I found myself in a hallway with fewer people--which meant I stood out.

"Should you be here?" a man asked, moving to block my way.

"Yes," I said, pulling out my badge again.

"You feds got here fast," the man said. "The lead detective is interviewing a witness now."

"Do you have many witnesses?" I asked.

"Only two survived."

Survived? "What's your name?"

"Chad."

"I'm Cassie. Can you walk me through what happened?"

"You'll probably want the detective for that."

"What he's doing is much more important than talking to me, I'm sure."

Chad shrugged. "From what we understand so far, four men came through the front door, through the vestibule and circled around the pews to this door. Two of the men are caucasian, one black, and one man had an unknown ethnicity."

"Unknown?"

"One of the witnesses say he was Asian, the other says Hispanic or Latino."

I nodded. Witness statements almost never lined up, which often made things confusing. At the same time, the commonalities between the stories might pinpoint aspects of the crime.

"One man stood by the door and the other three came down this hall. They went straight to the offices where the relics are kept."

"Did they take more than the thorn?"

"No. Everything else was left untouched. Unfortunately, three church officials were in the room. Two were murdered, and the other injured. Another priest heard yells and ran into the men in the hallway. The encounter earned him a nasty head wound and a trip to the hospital."

"These men went to where the thorn was kept. Do we know if someone inside the church helped them?"

"If we have any details about suspects assisting the intruders, it hasn't reached me yet. You'll need to talk to the detective to find out more."

Chad glanced away a few times, apparently eager to be elsewhere, so I thanked him for his time and wandered around a little more. I managed to eavesdrop on more conversations and one interview, but didn't gain any useful information.

The location where the relics were stored was tidy, aside from the blood. A few fallen papers and apparent evidence of a small scuffle, were the only notable indications of a disturbance.

Figuring a case file would fill in the blanks, I went in search of my partners and found them waiting for me outside.

"Did you learn anything?" I asked as I approached.

"Once they left the building they moved two blocks south and got into a vehicle," Rider said.

"How about you?" Logan asked.

I ran them through what I had learned while we walked back to the car.

"These guys were professionals," Logan said. "And it doesn't sound like they hesitated to kill."

"If it's the same group of people, their level of violence is escalating," I said.

"Two of them were at the shaman's house," Rider said. "The smells of the other two are unknown to me."

"And since that's the case, we've got a lot more to do today," Logan said. "Let's go to the other crime scenes. Maybe we can find out if the other thefts involved the team that hit the house and the church."

"If they aren't connected somehow, it's going to be a hell of a coincidence," I said.

"There's still a possibility that the crimes aren't related, but it's unlikely," Logan said. "We've got to find the connection between the items themselves."

"There is another question to consider," Rider said.

"What's that?" I asked.

"Why are the artifacts in this city?" Rider asked. "It would be surprising if each of these races keep antiquities like this here all the time. There are safer places."

"Good point," Logan said.

"And we already know at least two of the stolen relics were only in town temporarily," I said. "The shamans said the statue was passing through here on the way to somewhere else, and the Catholic Church's tour happened to be stopping here."

"The different people do not appear to have close contact with each other," Rider said. "We need to research, but I do not think the thefts were coordinated by the groups."

"But someone outside of the people affected could have orchestrated this," Logan said. "Possibly by someone who has influence over all of them."

I shifted uncomfortably. "The only ones I can think of with that type of knowledge are AIR and MyTH."

"There are others which possess a more subtle connection to the Lost and supernaturals," Logan said.

That didn't make me feel any better. "I'm going to call Taylor and see if he can reach out to the community. If more of these types of relics are around, they aren't safe."

Passing the message on to Taylor didn't take long, and he put Neil in charge of trying to find a common thread among the victims.

"I think we've been overlooking the power of the objects," I said.

"Only a few of them were used for actual rituals and such," Logan said. "They're powerful symbols to the owners."

"I mean the energy inside," I said. "We know souls are useful to others. We've seen them used before."

"Maybe, but you would need a Walker to take the soul out," Rider said. "And it does not work for the other thefts."

"I don't think they'd need to access the soul directly." Rider watched me, waiting for more. "These things have been around for ages, right?"

"Some of them may be thousands of years old," Logan said.

"And they were important to a group of people," I continued. "They concentrated on the relic, sought power from them, worshiped them, or have just generally used the items."

"That is the case," Rider agreed.

Logan nodded and appeared to follow my train of thought, which encouraged me. "The artifacts probably soaked up energy which some people might be able to use. For example, as a Reader, I could use the Path to take strength out of any of them. Not the soul, but the power behind it. As a point of focus for the races, I imagine each artifact stored strength from the people around them."

"Witches could use them like that," Logan said. "There are a few others as well. It's an odd mixture of energy, though."

"Has anything else happened that would gather or expend a large amount of power?" I asked.

"The portal mentioned," Rider said. "It did not open correctly, but that would need a lot of energy."

"There may be more to it," Logan said. "Some of these artifacts were stolen before the portal stutter. Some of them after."

"Three thefts have occurred in a very short period of time," Rider said. "And all three were stolen since the first portal incident."

"So, if someone's using the power, they started with three items, and now they have doubled the count," Logan said.

"I think we should go to the portal sight," I said. "We might be able to find out more about what happened. It's possible the activity isn't connected."

"It'll be good to rule it out," Logan said. "Today we're seeing the druids, so we'll put off the portal visit until tomorrow and go first thing in the morning."

"If someone did use the stolen items, will their power be gone?" Rider asked. "Or can it be rebuilt?"

"It's hard to say," Logan said. "I guess it depends on the artifact."

"The original owners may not need the forces inside," I said. "For some, it might just be a symbol. Potent yes, but maybe they don't use the energy."

"That *will* be the case for at least some of them," Logan said. "There's still the possibility that the artifacts aren't being drained. Someone could be selling them."

"Or collecting them for themselves," Rider said. "If they are rich enough to buy something like this, they could arrange for the thefts to begin with."

"Someone with the money and knowledge of the people and objects could also wield influence over the races. If someone is subtly maneuvering the parties involved, they could have lured the items here," Logan said. "You may be on to something."

THE VISIT TO THE DRUIDS' house where the piece of charred wood had been stolen only added more questions to the problem, while offering no solutions. Two of the thieves involved at other crime scenes and two others hadn't.

Back at MyTH Rider sought out Angel, and Logan turned in early, which left me alone, wandering the empty halls. Even when I went to the clinic, I found the large room eerily vacant, but I didn't want to be by myself. With no one around my mind turned to Vincent; I had no way to help him return to our world, so it did no good to dwell on those thoughts.

Keeping busy was key.

To my relief, Neil's lab was in its usual disorganized state, with Neil himself at his computer scrolling through information at a speed I couldn't follow. Smoke wafted up from the ashtray beside him and it wasn't the scent of cigarettes filling the air.

"Searching for connections between the races?" I asked. "How's it going?"

Neil picked up his joint and took a hit before answering. "It's maddening, but I'll be better in a few minutes."

"I guess the number of people involved doesn't help," I said. "Each crime scene had multiple thieves."

"With two constants, that part was easy. They're professionals, probably hiring out some of the work."

"Professional what?"

Neil shrugged. "Crooks, goons, killers. They're expert bad guys. What I can't make sense of is who's connecting them."

"I'm surprised someone would hire the jobs out this way. Why trust so many people?"

"For some people it's easier to work with many than trusting one. Bring in an individual and they may realize what you're doing and try to take the stuff for themselves. Hiring different people that aren't aware of each other... well, what's a piece of charred wood to an average thief?"

"I see what you mean."

Neil proffered the joint, but I declined and sat down at his work bench, trying to find meaning in the clutter that amassed around him. My name was written on the top folder, so I flipped it open.

It was almost disappointing to see my brain scans.

"Dude, I can't get anywhere with that either. It, like, doesn't make sense." He slid the file over to himself and choose two different images to stare at.

I sighed. "That's what I get for shredding my soul."

"What do you mean?"

"Taylor didn't tell you?"

"He, like, tried to talk to me earlier, but I think he wound up pissed off. The feeling was mutual."

"Oh." Where do you start with something like this?

In the end, I started with the gremlins' concoction and ended with my discovery while meditating.

"Dude, that is messed up."

"It is." I sighed and stared blankly at the image of my brain.

"But it totally brings a sort of logic to all of this. Well, almost everything, anyway."

"I'm glad you see it, because I don't."

"Before, the pieces of your soul slid around each other. Even when the other pieces joined yours, they glided around. They didn't, like, mess with the harmony of it all."

"Harmony? I guess that's one way of looking at it."

"Now," Neil said, not paying me any attention, "those gremlins bonded that shit together. When you broke it apart again, it's still, like, trying to make random connections. Your soul is banging into itself." He pulled out my scans and took another drag. "The tranquility was ruined, man."

"When I look inside, there's chaos."

"What about the other souls?"

"Pieces," I reminded him, worried about how broken I sounded. "There are fewer of them than before. Vincent was able to release some of them. Most of the others, though, melded with my own. They're a part of me now. Some fragments hang out off to the side on their own."

"Dude."

I waited for more, but I was the one to break the silence. "Any idea how to fix it?"

"Without, like, reverse engineering what the gremlins did, your soul won't get put back together. Who even thought it would be possible to rebuild in the first place?"

"I'm not sure I want it back to normal." I struggled to find the words to explain how I felt, so I ended up stealing what Neil had said. "I just want the harmony back."

"I think you're, like, on the right track with meditation. I'll research it, but if you concentrate on letting those shards glide past each other again, you'll be golden." He picked up the scan of my brain lit up like a Christmas tree on steroids. "I'm pretty sure all the pain is your soul's way of, like, being heard."

"That makes sense." At least in a way it did.

"When you're all, like, emotional and shit, your soul gets

all worked up and freaks out. My advice is to start the day with a little weed and meditation. Take a nice chill afternoon break with a joint, and end your day mellowed out with friends."

"I think that would just make me crave ding-dongs and sleep."

Neil jumped up and went to his fridge. "Dude! Ding-dongs! Those are the shit." He rummaged around for a while and looked disappointed when he came back with chips.

"Thanks for the advice, though," I said. "Reflecting on the issue and hanging out with people might do the trick."

"That's cool."

"In fact, I think I'll go meditate before turning in." I took one sad glance at the folder before taking my leave.

MEDITATION WAS ABOUT AS useful as it had been the last time. When I tried to concentrate on shifting around the pieces of my soul, Vincent sprang to mind and I kept losing control. Once again, I felt dejected.

After tossing and turning all night, I didn't want to face the following day. Figuring that mainlining caffeine was going to be the only way to get me moving, I went to the kitchen, where I found Rider. His face was downcast, which caused immediate worry.

"What's wrong?" I asked.

Rider didn't look up. "Have you spoken to Logan this morning?"

"No. Why? Did he hear something? Did something happen to Vincent?"

"Vincent has not been in contact. I am sure he will call you when he is able."

I downplayed my concern. "What's up, then?"

"Logan is going to the Farm."

"He's going? Why?"

"Hank and I think it's the best move," Logan said, walking in.

"Why? Do we know what's going on at the office?" I asked.

"They're pressing down on Kyrian pretty hard to call us in," Logan said. "If I go, it'll placate them for a while."

"Should I go with you?" I asked.

"No," Logan said with more emphasis than expected. "Not a chance. The doc has your back."

"It seems like it would be easier to just go in and answer their questions." When Logan didn't reply, I started to worry. "Unless there's something you aren't telling me." Still, he said nothing. "Logan?"

He shifted uncomfortably. "There are some visitors with high clearance. They went through your records."

"So. Why should that matter?" I asked.

"Vincent tried to kill you."

"But that was a mistake."

"We know it was, but a lot of the documents were redacted. With the information left it looks bad."

"What does that have to do with what's going on now?"

"News around the office is that Washington thinks you took Vincent out."

My mouth dropped open and my mind went blank aside from the accusation. "They can't really think..." My chest felt like it was being squeezed. "Our co-workers, they don't believe..."

"They don't," Logan said. "Which is the main reason you haven't been arrested."

"Arrested?" I squeaked.

"Kyrian put her foot down, but it's causing her position to be a bit shaky with the higher ups," Logan said.

My breathing became short and sharp.

"Don't panic," Logan said. "Vincent will be back, and then the subject will be dropped."

Rider came over and placed a hand on my shoulder. "He will return soon."

Before, I had wanted Vincent to make it back to ensure he was okay. Now, though, I needed him back so I could avoid a prison sentence.

"And no one at the office--"

"Paulson is especially adamant. He's still head of the investigation on our end."

"On our end?" I asked.

"This case crosses branches, so the true leads are from the main office."

Logan and I couldn't have been the only people under the microscope. "Was Boone able to leave?"

"They didn't have the authority to detain him for further questions," Logan said. "Whatever project he's working on is apparently big enough or important enough to give him a get-out-of-jail-free card."

What is Boone doing?

"I don't think Boone would have left if he knew they'd be gunning for you," Logan added.

"Probably not."

"If he's got some pull, maybe you can call him and--"

"No. I don't want to drag him back here," I said. "Besides, like you both said, Vincent will be home soon."

"The sooner the better." It wasn't the first time Logan had said those words, and it made me wonder how long he'd suspected something like this might happen. "Don't let the out-of-towners worry you. No one's bringing you in on charges yet. Until that happens, Taylor can keep them off your back."

How could I not be unsettled while being a murder suspect?

"Besides, you two have work today," Logan said. "Between Rider's nose and reading, you might be able find out if someone tried to open a portal using our missing artifacts."

"Shouldn't we wait for you?" I asked.

"No," Logan said. "Talk to Taylor. Maybe he's got some ideas on what else you could check for while you're out there."

Logan tipped his hat to us and left, which ratcheted up my anxiety.

Rider detoured to his room while I went in search of Taylor. Concentrating on the case was the only thing that might keep me distracted.

Before I reached my destination, Neil found me. He was wide eyed and fidgety.

"Long night?" I asked.

"Yeah, man, Taylor has me putting together some equipment," Neil said.

"I was heading to his office."

"Same here. We're about to make headway on who's the man with the plan."

"What?" I asked, already feeling a step behind.

"The person behind the thefts. There's a good chance we'll flush him out by the end of the week."

"How are we going to do that?"

"We found another artifact nearby. Taylor's like, negotiating security and checking in with Gordon."

"Who owns it?"

"The witches. It's like, part of another world."

"Are we sure someone will steal it?"

"As far as we know, they haven't done anything with what they've taken so far. We've already started floating a rumor that the relic is being moved out of town tomorrow and we're providing the honor guard."

"So, if they aren't already aware of the object, they should know about it now."

"And if someone wants it bad enough, they have to come get it."

If I were the crook behind this, knowing that MyTH was on to me would make me lay low. "What makes you think they'll risk it if they know MyTH is helping?"

"They're willing to kill priests to get this shit. There's, like, eternal damnation in a special kind of hell for murdering a holy man. A few agents and office workers aren't going to scare them."

"Good point."

We found Taylor at his desk studying a tablet.

"Morning," I said with a falsely cheery voice. "Logan told me you might have some ideas for us today, and Neil filled me in.

"Is Logan still here?" Taylor asked.

There was no way to even fake being happy while saying Logan was gone. "He's already on his way back to the Farm."

"We need to push forward our time table," Taylor said.

"Why the rush?" I asked.

"If the thefts haven't been reported to AIR, they will be soon, especially if this doesn't work," Taylor said. "I'm not sure how much attention they'll give the issue, though."

"Since this happened in the city, won't they call MyTH before they send any agents out?" I asked.

Taylor shook his head. "After the calls I've received today, I'm not so sure."

"Like, how bad are they?" Neil asked.

"They're threatening sanctions," Taylor said.

"What?" I squeaked.

"I'm sure they're hollow threats," Taylor said.

I wished he appeared as confident as he sounded.

"I should go into the office," I said.

"You can't risk it," Taylor said. "If you do, Logan's not certain you'll be released until Vincent resurfaces."

The situation turned my stomach into knots. "This is getting out of hand."

"Let's wait until we hear more before we worry," Taylor said. "Listen, I've got some of your test results. Why don't we go over those?"

He couldn't hide the fact he was making a desperate attempt to change the subject.

Life was becoming too much. "I'll meet up with you all later."

I walked out, not giving either of them a chance to say anything. I heard Neil and Taylor talking, but I didn't slow down to listen.

I went to my room, trying to keep my mind empty. From there I went into the bathroom and locked the door. It was only then that I let everything crash over me.

Possible murder charges loomed in my future, but I had a hard time envisioning myself in jail. I needed Vincent to come home, and now there was unexpected guilt wrapped around the thought. I'd wanted him to come safely home, but my freedom had become tied to his return in a very real way.

Was it bad that my wanting him back had morphed into being desperate to have him back?

Someone knocked on the door.

"I'll meet up with you in a little while," I called, turning on the sink.

"It is me," Rider said.

"I need a few minutes."

"Neil thought you might. That is why I am here." He settled down on the floor outside the room.

I hesitated, then dampened a cloth and joined him from my side, putting my back against the door. I knew voicing my concerns would make me overly emotional, so I didn't. Instead, I sat quietly. At first I thought about Vincent, but that dragged my mood even further down. Then my mind skipped to the office. It took me a while to sort that out in my head. In the end, the people at work were being ridiculous. I knew what I did, and my coworkers trusted me. Only the out-of-towners thought I was responsible for something sinister and who cared what they thought?

Then came the problems with my powers and the pathetic state my soul was in. As those thoughts entered my head, I realized out of all my issues, fixing myself was the only thing I could do anything about, so I closed my eyes and began to meditate.

Twenty minutes later, I felt better. Nothing had changed, at least not outwardly, but mentally I was sure I could face the rest of the day. I decided that the gremlin concoction would wear off, which would probably help immensely in the effort to control my power again.

And the team from Washington could go screw themselves. The important people, my family and friends, knew the truth. No one else mattered.

The biggest hurdle was the one I couldn't quite cross. My worry for Vincent grew. Trying to remind myself that he could handle himself didn't help. The idea that he knew how to get in and out between the worlds seemed flimsy, since he hadn't made it back.

The tears that had fallen were gone so I took a deep breath and got off the floor. I barely glanced in the mirror before splashing water on my face. Once I dried off I forced myself back into the outside world.

I opened the door and was immediately engulfed by Rider. The act was another unexpected event for the day, but a good one. He hugged me and I smiled, hugging him back.

"I'm okay," I said after a while.

"I know that you are, but I am worried."

"Don't be, I'm fine. I just needed a few minutes."

"I am not sure that there is anything I can do to help."

"You just did. More than I can say."

"If you are arrested--"

"I won't be." I found it easier to assure Rider than to convince myself. "And meditating with me will be a big help." I stepped back and looked up at my friend. He appeared anxious. "I think with Logan gone, it's going to be a long day."

Rider nodded.

Now that I had my resolve sorted out, I could tell I wasn't the only one having trouble coming to grips with everything happening.

"Meditating is really going to help me," I said. "I think I can realign my soul somehow."

Rider smiled. "We will both feel better once your powers are back on track."

"Agreed. Now, I think it is time to see Taylor."

CHAPTER
EIGHT

"Come in," Taylor called when I knocked. "I thought I'd examine your stiches while we go over your test results."

I stared at my arm. The attack at the AIR offices seemed a lifetime ago, instead of just a few days. "Is the office asking for an update?"

"Something like that. It's nothing to worry about."

I raised my eyebrow, giving him an incredulous look.

"If Logan doesn't come back tonight, then you can start worrying."

Is that a possibility?

Taylor must have seen the reaction on my face. "There's no way they're going to hold Logan. You seem more bothered than I've ever seen you. Don't be. This will all blow over."

"Sure."

"I didn't examine your arm before," Taylor said, changing the subject. "Rider, would you mind going to help Neil load our equipment?"

Rider nodded. "And I will not listen in."

"Thank you," Taylor said, seemingly embarrassed. Once Rider left, Taylor turned back to me, appearing to have something weighing heavily on his mind. "Okay, your arm. How bad were you hurt?"

"I didn't need many stitches. Rider was injured much worse than me."

"Not everyone can heal like him. Don't be in a rush." Taylor unwrapped my arm. "As for your other issue, your blood work does show an abnormality. So far, the tests to determine the nature of the irregularity have been inconclusive. The gremlin medicine could still be in your system."

"I'm not sure I'd call that stuff medicine."

Taylor began to carefully clean the area around the stitches. "Until we figure out what we're looking at, there's nothing we can do to counteract it."

"It could be dissipating, though, right?"

"That's a possibility."

"Is there any way to check? I know Dr. Yelton took blood samples when I got back. He said something odd showed up in them."

"If there was a pressing need, I would make the request. I'm afraid if we ask for prior results right now, Dr. Yelton could be pressured to bring you in for their own exams."

"These people invading the office are really aggravating."

Taylor smiled, but looked as though he tried not to. "I don't understand how this foreign material in your system could affect what you see in the Path. What you described might explain the headaches, but not the changes in what's seen."

"The first time my soul was shattered the shapes of the pieces were all sharply pointed; like cut diamonds or something. This time everything is curved, and something is trying to draw the parts together. It's the only difference I've seen."

"I wish there was some research we could do in this area, but you are unique."

"That's a nice way of putting it."

"We'll keep looking," Taylor said. "In the meantime, your stitches will be ready to come out soon."

"Good. Having thread sewn into my skin freaks me out."

Taylor laughed and started to re-wrap my arm. "Are you keeping up with your self-defense training?"

It was my turn to laugh. "Not exactly. Boone and I sparred while we were stuck in the gremlin world, but I haven't done anything more in weeks. Before that I was doing well, though."

"Were you that bored in the other world? That it came down to sparring?"

Some of my smile faltered, but I managed to keep at least part of it. "We didn't have the chance to get bored. Boone wanted to get an idea of what I could do. The fight with the creature we faced was more offense than defense, which I kind of suck at."

"I imagine your classes don't deal much with offensive training."

"No. And the few times that you and I have gotten together, we've never worked on attacking beyond what's needed to subdue someone enough to get away."

"I try not to practice purposefully hurting someone."

"I don't blame you. It feels... strange. I imagine as a doctor, it's worse."

Taylor didn't say anything.

"What made you decide to go into medicine?" I asked.

"It was past time for me to help people."

I waited, expecting more.

"You never told your partners that I'm not human, did you?"

"Um, when we first met I didn't know it was a secret. I

mentioned to Rider that I didn't think you were. He said you smelled human, so I let it drop."

Taylor looked uncomfortable about that. "He never said anything?"

"Why should he?"

"I thought Logan or Rider would want to know more about who they're working with, but no one asked."

"If you want to tell me, you will. If not, you don't have to. It doesn't change anything either way."

"Maybe. Before I became a doctor, I followed a different way of life. A much more... aggressive one."

It was a little hard to picture Taylor hurting anyone, even after sparring with him.

"In the medical profession I have a chance to make up for at least a small part of my past."

"Well, I consider myself very lucky you're a doctor. You've helped me with things I never thought I'd see."

"Hopefully you won't experience them again. Maybe in a few weeks, once your arm is better, we can add on to your self-defense training. If you're interested, that is."

"Are you sure you don't mind doing something like that?"

"To be honest, I have some concerns over what you're seeing in the Path. If any other beings live there, I want to help you gain the tools necessary to fight if there ever becomes a need. It especially wouldn't hurt with some of the creatures you come up against in the normal course of your work."

"I'm not going to have to attack you, am I?"

"That's generally the way sparring goes. One person attacks, then the other, or you both attack at once."

I curled my nose up, not liking the idea. "I'll give it a shot, but I promise nothing in terms of results. What's the plan for today?"

"We're going to meet with Angel and we'll trade places

standing guard throughout the day and night. Neil has equipment to help us out if it's needed."

"Do you think rumors of moving the object will lure them in?"

"I'm almost certain they'll try, but it depends on how badly someone wants what the witches have."

"What kind of security is in place, aside from us?"

"Almost nothing," Taylor said. "The item is at someone's house, much like the others. We have ourselves and anything that Neil has cooked up."

"What does Neil have?"

"Honestly, it's hard to say. He's constantly tinkering with equipment. Every now and again one of his drugs makes him paranoid and he comes up with some new alarm system or monitoring device."

I tried not to smile. "Somehow I can picture that. Vividly."

"There are a few entrances that are easier targets than others. We're observing remotely now, but Angel is our only real security on site."

"Tell me where you want me and I'll be there."

Taylor looked hesitant. "What is the likelihood you'd stay in your room tonight?"

I grinned. "Zero."

He shook his head. "I thought as much, but I had to ask. You'll mostly be with Neil."

"While he's on guard duty?"

"He won't be guarding. Not physically, anyway. He'll be in the van."

"It sounds like there's very little chance I'll be useful to Neil."

"You asked where I wanted you," Taylor reminded me. "Besides, you're the only one that can put up with Neil for long periods of time and I don't want him left alone."

"I'll be there," I said, figuring I was lucky that he wasn't threatening to lock me up somewhere.

"Get what you need for the next twenty-four hours," Taylor said. "We leave in an hour and it's likely to be a long night."

ONCE WE ARRIVED, Neil set to work with Angel's help. I spent that time in the house, guarding what appeared to be a glass vial filled with tar.

Before dark, Taylor gave everyone a position and orders. Rider, Angel, and Jonathan were in the woods at the edges of the property while Taylor stood guard inside. Neil and I found ourselves in the van, locked up tight. Neil sat on the van's floor, monitoring security cameras on a tablet, and a bank of monitors while I checked my phone every other minute to see if Logan or Vincent was trying to call.

"Partnered up again," Neil said. "No worries. I've got your back."

"Thanks," I said. "And I've got yours."

"Dude, security's tight, so we can, like, chill.

"What did you set up?" I asked.

"Cameras, motion detectors, smoke bombs, trip wires, small explosives--"

"You put explosives in their house?"

"Not in their house," Neil said. "Outside. Taylor and everyone else on guard knows what to expect. Besides, the charge is so small that a bottle rocket is more dangerous. It's just to alert us to where they are and hopefully throw our thieves off some."

I joined Neil on the floor, sitting cross legged. "It sounds like you have everything covered."

"Yeah, so, like, we can kick back. I've got solitaire if you want to take it for a spin."

"Thanks, but I think I'll try meditating again."

"Cool. Be all mellow and let your soul flow. I've got some shrooms if you think it'd help."

"Thanks for the offer, but we should keep a clear head, just in case."

"Sure, man. I get it. I'll keep an eye on the monitors."

Any anxiety about the mission leaked away when I settled into a comfortable position. I closed my eyes and stretched my mind, reaching for the dark abyss waiting for me.

Mentally, I winced at seeing fragments crash around creating chaos. Some shards clung together, stretching out then springing back, slamming into other pieces. Instead of focusing on the whole mess, I focused on the linked parts, which appeared to cause all the problems.

It didn't make sense for some aspects of my soul to try hard to break away from parts they were stuck to, but that was the biggest problem. Concentrating on my breath and striving for gentle serenity, I nudged the fragments together while trying to prevent them from stretching away again. When I had those aligned, like a splash into a lake, ripples ran through the rest.

It wasn't perfect, but the shards weren't clashing so violently.

As they always do when my mind was blank, my thoughts went toward the missing Vincent, which caused worry to break into my calm. Once again, fragments bounced against each other, although not as hard as they previously had. I eased my focus away, concentrating only on the flow, ignoring all else until remnants fell into place.

"Dude, I think there's something wrong."

Neil's voice broke through. I had no idea how long I had sat there, but I felt as though I had a grip on my power for the first time in days.

"What do you mean?" I asked, opening my eyes slowly, worried I would internally break something again.

"Taylor looks anxious, which usually--"

Firecrackers snapped and popped outside.

"Which usually isn't a good thing when shits about to go down," Neil finished. He stayed intent on the computer screen which cast a forlorn glow in the dark space.

"Is anything happening that you can see?" I asked.

"No. There's, like, nothing I can see. Rider is running toward the noise, but Angel and Jonathan are just hanging out, more or less. Taylor's looking pretty intense though."

I tried to keep an eye on all the screens at once. "Why is Taylor being anxious so important?"

"He's got, like, spidey sense."

It was my turn to give Neil an incredulous look. "What's that supposed to mean?"

"He senses it when bad shit is on the way, just like Spider-man. He says it has to do with the flow of natural energy or some shit."

"Does he get an idea of what's going to happen?"

"He wouldn't discuss it further," Neil said. "The only reason I know is because I worked it out on my own."

"Maybe he'll talk now. Ask him what's going on."

Neil turned on his comms. "Hey, man, what's happening?"

There was no reply.

"Hello?" Neil took out his ear-piece for inspection. "It looks okay. Is yours working?"

"Taylor?" I called through my comms.

"I'm not even picking you up. Let me try something else." Neil went to work on his laptop.

"Don't lose the video feeds," I said as I drew my weapon. "Keep an eye on them."

"I'll keep them on these screens," Neil said, pointing them out. He worked using the other monitors.

"We just lost Angel's camera." There was a hint of panic in Neil's voice, and his fingers flew furiously over the keyboard.

I moved enough to see around him, stealing quick glances of his screen while trying to watch our friends activity. On the monitor that showed Taylor, a blinding flash of light erupted and appeared to strike the camera directly.

Then Neil's computer went blank.

"Shit, shit, shit!" Neil tossed the laptop aside and jumped up. The whir of the equipment hadn't died away by the time he had a tablet out.

"Neil?" I called, peeking out through the blackened windows. "Do we have anything?"

"Everything's fried!" Neil grabbed yet another laptop and jabbed the power button.

"What could do that?"

He pulled things out of his pockets--string, a wallet, some coins and a baggie which probably contained something illegal. "EMP, lightning, virus--Look, there's a lot of possibilities that could 'in theory' kill the electronics." He pulled out a key ring. "But I don't think we're dealing with anything like those." Neil turned to a box which was bolted to the floor and unlocked it. He dragged out a heavy contraption which took me a few moments to recognize as an old portable computer. Not a laptop. This machine looked like it would crush any lap it sat on.

"Any idea what did cause this?" I asked.

Neil had a frantic erratic energy around him. He started his machine and a small screen flickered to life. "Hard to say, but we've been left blind. And whatever's going on, there's a good chance it's happening to Taylor right now. You need to go help him."

The thought had occurred to me as well. I wanted to jump out of the van and run down the short road to the house and help Taylor. The idea was a reckless one, though.

"Taylor knows what he's doing," I said. "And I'm pretty sure Rider is on his way."

Neil concentrated on lines of green code that scrolled down on what appeared to be the only working computer he had access to. He attached an archaic keyboard and started typing again. Soon the screen showed a few evenly spaced horizontal and vertical lines in a grid and a blinking dash.

"It hasn't moved," Neil said.

"What hasn't?" I asked, not connecting the dots.

"The witch's relic. It's still there. Taylor must be okay, then."

Neil didn't sound convinced and I wasn't about to rely on a computer that looked as though it belonged in a museum.

"Stay inside the van," I said. "I'm stepping outside, but I'll be right next to the door. If Taylor needs help, I'm more likely to hear him from out there."

"I'm going to try to find out what's happening here," Neil said. "We need to see what's going on."

"We do what we can from here." As quietly as I could, I opened the door, stepped out, and gently pushed the door closed.

The night was quiet. If it weren't for the earlier alerts, it would feel like any peaceful night in the country. The stars were bright and small breezes danced around. Everything was normal.

"It's moving," Neil called.

The van door banged open and Neil jumped out. He

dragged the ancient computer over and jabbed a finger at the screen. "They've got it."

"Shhh," I hissed, trying to get my friend to calm down.

A shot erupted, destroying any hope that Neil hadn't been heard.

There was no way for me to know which direction the sound came from or if the gun had been aimed at us. I threw myself at Neil and we both fell to the ground. Skin stretched away from the stitches in my arm causing me to suck in a sharp breath, but the pain was momentary.

Without risking the time to take a short meditation, I jumped into the Path. What little mental work I had done earlier made a difference. My head pounded, but it wasn't debilitating. I looked and felt around the Path, sensing for movement. People approached fast on two sides.

I scrambled to my feet and solidified the air around us as best I could. Working with the Path scorched my mind, but I kept hold.

My brain started to catch up. Both of the Paths approaching were familiar. Taylor came into view before I had time to release my power.

"Neil!" Taylor cried out.

Looking down at where I left Neil, he appeared stunned, but otherwise okay.

Taylor dropped to his knees and started to look over Neil.

"He's okay," I said, trying to assure Taylor.

"He is not bleeding," came Rider's voice from the darkness.

"Dude," Neil said, pushing at one of Taylor's hands. "I'm okay. She like, jumped on me when we heard the gun."

"You shouldn't even be out of the van," Taylor said. He didn't sound as frantic as he had, but when he glared at me, his aggravation was scrawled across his face.

"Comms, were down, man," Neil said, sitting up. "Cassie

was like, standing guard, and I jumped out to give her an update."

"Right," Taylor said, tight lipped. "You're both okay?"

"Sure man," Neil said. "But what happened?"

"We lost the artifact," Taylor said.

CHAPTER

NINE

Something in the vehicle beeped and a whirring noise followed.

Neil jumped up. "I was just telling Cassie that the relic is on the move." He poked his head into the van. "Electronics are starting back up. If they haven't completely shorted out, we should have comms again soon."

"What do we do now?" Rider asked. "I tracked their trail for a short way, but they had vehicle."

Neil jumped into the van. "Dude, the witches are going to be pissed if we lost their stuff. They can do some nasty shit when they're mad. We have to follow the thieves."

Taylor hurried to the driver's door. "You have a signal from the relic?"

"Of course man. If things went wrong I didn't want to, like, wake up as a frog or something."

"Get in," Taylor said. "Call Angel and Johnathan and tell them to lock up and join us when they can."

Rider slid into the passenger side while I joined Neil in the back.

Neil was in his element again. Within a few keystrokes he started giving directions.

"When they reach a main road, we'll have a better idea of where they're going," Neil said. "They're moving fast."

"I do not know anything about witches," Rider said. "Can they turn people into frogs?"

"He was exaggerating," Taylor said.

"That is good," Rider said.

"There are only two or three witches in the world with enough strength and skill to transform someone," Taylor continued.

"But they could easily make us think we were frogs," Neil said.

Rider cast an anxious look at Neil. "I do not know which is worse."

"The witches aren't going to come after us," I said. "We know where their artifact is. We follow our thieves, and take it back."

"Hopefully we'll find the other stolen relics at the same time," Taylor said.

I frowned and wondered if that had been a part of the plan all along. If it was, I missed the memo. "What happened inside?"

Taylor cleared his throat. "I'm not exactly sure. There was something...off in the room."

"Spidey sense, man," Neil said.

Taylor rolled his eyes and shook his head. "I was alert and before long the atmosphere of the room changed."

"How so?" I asked.

"The room grew... thin. It was almost as if the air left the room. It became difficult to breath and I'm not sure what happened next. One moment the relic was there and the next it disappeared."

"It was just gone?" I asked.

"That's all I saw. Something had to have happened."

"Maybe the lack of oxygen actually, like, knocked you out for a minute or something?" Neil said.

"It's possible. How close are we?" Taylor asked, changing the focus of discussion.

"They're turning onto the interstate," Neil said. "Moving north."

"They're not going to the city then," Taylor said.

"Is that a good thing or a bad thing?" Rider asked.

"There are more people around in the city," Taylor said. "If things go bad, there is less of a chance of any innocent bystanders getting in the way."

"They can't disappear no matter where they are," Neil said. "Well, the relic can't. We should be able to track it anywhere."

"Will they notice the bug?" I asked

"Not likely," Neil said. "There was wax around the cork. I melted a little and put the tracker there."

"They likely won't mess with the cork," Taylor said.

"Unless they need to open the bottle to use the power," Rider said.

"I don't think they'll have to," I said. "They wouldn't be able to open the statue or charred wood. Definitely not the diamond. I think they just need the artifacts themselves."

"We still do not have any idea who might use these objects," Rider said.

As we traveled, following Neil's directions, we discussed Lost, humans, and supernaturals. After twenty or thirty minutes, we were no closer to an answer. The tracker stopped moving at one point, but moved again before we caught up.

"So," Rider said, "we know there are many races capable of using the objects, but we are not sure who they are."

"And we don't know who could have affected the room

Taylor was in earlier," I added. "It would help if we knew if it's the energy they're after or the items themselves."

"We'll know for sure soon," Neil said. "In fact, I'm ninety-two point seven percent sure they're using the relics as a power source."

"What makes you so certain?" Rider asked.

"Because they left the interstate," Neil said. "They're heading in the same direction the portal stuttered a few days ago."

"Why would they need artifacts for a portal?" Rider asked. "Why not use the same source AIR does?"

"The amount of electricity needed would attract AIR, even before the portal opened," Neil said. "Then they'd like, get involved."

"But they would notice this as well," Rider said.

"Only once the portal is open, or as it's opening," Taylor said. "AIR doesn't deal with anything which resembles magic."

"Why wouldn't they?" I asked. "It doesn't make sense to me." In a way it did though. My belief that magic could be real was only on the surface. Deep in my bones, I wasn't sure. There could be another explanation.

"I think it's outside of their wheelhouse," Taylor said. "They operate within certain parameters. They bring specific mythological creatures into this world, find the ones that accidentally wander here, send them home when they can, and keep them all a secret. But there's more to our world than Lost and humans. Some of it they may not know about, believe in, or just plain don't care about because it's not their job."

"You'd think they'd worry about the secret of the Lost getting out if, let's say, people found out magic is real," I said. "Who's monitoring supernaturals to make sure they aren't discovered"

"Dude, they monitor themselves," Neil said. "Historically not well, but it mostly works."

"What do you mean, not so well?" Rider asked.

"Witches were decimated, like, almost totally wiped out, multiple times in history. Werewolves and vampires were hunted," Neil said. "Anything which wasn't seen as regular run-of-the-mill human has been targeted."

"Along with some regular run-of-the-mill humans," Taylor said.

"Yeah. People aren't very tolerant," Neil said. "It should be, like, mandatory to smoke a bowl in the morning and chill out before you start the day."

"I do not see that happening," Rider said.

"A lot of mythological creatures are still seen as mythological," Taylor said. "Even to AIR the Chinese dragons, djinn, and countless others, they aren't seen anymore. Not that I know of anyway."

"You mean, they were here and hunted to extinction," I said.

"Sometimes it's not that hard, man," Neil said. "Like, if only one hell hound gets into this world and the portal's gone again, killing one makes it extinct here. The handful of witnesses would still spread it around. And the stories, like, get distorted throughout time."

"It's like what you said when we first met. Everything exists somewhere," I said. "It's sad to hear what we've done ."

"It is," Taylor said. "Think of all we could have learned. Medicines could have progressed further, we'd be more aware of some exotic animals and plants. Instead, throughout history for valor, victory, self-pride, or for the whim of some emperor, we've killed."

"Is your world similar to this, Rider?" I asked.

"Yes and no," Rider said as we pulled off the interstate with a line of other cars. "People are extremely territorial in my world. If the interloper is aggressive, they will be met with aggression. If they are not hostile or assertive then they might be welcomed or left alone. As long as they don't try to stake a claim in certain areas, there were no battles. Instead, we fought each other."

"They're pulling off the main roads now," Neil said. "They're going to some park. Or going through it at least."

"What's the plan?" I asked. "Are we just going to jump out and take back the items? Do we arrest them? I'm not sure what to do since I'm not on the job."

"I'll handle that part," Taylor said. "I know who to call to help us out."

"Someone in AIR?" Rider asked.

"No," Taylor said. "AIRs not going to care too much since it's stolen artifacts we're dealing with. Everyone has filed a police report, though. We'll get these guys arrested for theft and murder. Once we take them down and have them safely bundled up, we'll make a citizen's arrest, more or less. I'll call the right officials and they'll make the actual arrest."

"There are cops that know what the score is?" I asked.

"Certainly," Taylor said. "There are police from every walk of life. There are a few that are highly interested in seeing these people behind bars because of what they've done to the supernatural community."

"Should we involve them ahead of time?" Rider asked.

"I thought about it," Taylor said. He glanced at me in the rear view mirror. "It's best to not involve anyone outside of MyTH or ourselves if we don't have to."

"Yeah," Neil said. "We don't want the man coming down on us and screwing things up."

Or taking me away, I thought morosely. Involving officials means AIR could hear about me running around tracking thieves and murderers. If they knew, they'd haul me in no matter what Taylor told them.

"They've stopped on the other side of the park," Neil said. "There's a house or something, but it sits away from the road quite a bit. At least according to the satellite pictures."

"Are there any places nearby which might be a good place to stop?" Taylor asked.

"I'll check some areas out," Neil said.

"I'll pull over up here at the gas station and we can look at the maps to find a good route," Taylor said.

"If we drive up to the house, do you think they will run?" Rider asked.

"We can't take the chance," Taylor said. "Neil, pull up everything you can find about the property and owner."

Taylor parked at the station and climbed into the back with Neil to discuss our approach. I tried to look over their shoulders at first, but it felt too crowded.

Since they knew the area better than me, I watched people fill their gas tanks and tried some deep breathing and meditation, but without closing my eyes. It was surprisingly easy to zone out while watching everyone around us.

A few of the cars from the interstate also pulled into the station. Two filled their tanks and were on their way again, one couple got out and wandered inside, and another vehicle, much like us, had pulled over and seemed to be doing something in their car.

All these people, going about their daily routines--none of them aware of the real world around them.

It wasn't something I thought of often, but what must it be like for them to live in a world where so much was invisible to them? Throughout history, each time society caught a hint of something out of the ordinary, they attacked, so it's obviously better they don't know about the hidden world.

I was privy to a lot of it, and still there were things which surprised me every day. Like magic. Who would have guessed magic existed? I mean, sure, I had Frank for a while and I'm sure there's no way to get a zombie bunny without a little magic. But witches? Druids? Even working for AIR I only see a small part of what's happening around me. I wondered what else was out there. What haven't I heard about yet? What will I learn tomorrow?

"I think we have a plan," Taylor said, breaking into my meditation. "It looks like there's only one road into this place, so we're going to block the main driveway. We'll approach on foot from there. Neil's going to wait in the van. He'll alert us to anything we need to be aware of."

"And for the rest of us?" I asked.

"I think Rider should get into position behind the house before we move in. He can stay in the woods and let us know if anything happens. He's also the best suited to quietly approach. It's getting dark, but the house is supposed to be abandoned, so we don't know if they'll be inside or out."

"And you and I?" I asked, silently hoping since he hadn't mentioned me yet, I wouldn't be waiting in the van with Neil.

"We walk up and knock on the door." Taylor got back in the driver's seat and we were once again on our way. "How is your head feeling?"

"You mean, 'can I read'," I said. "The pain isn't as bad as it was before. Neil gave me some advice, and it seems to be working. I'm still not one hundred percent back on form, but I can manage this way without pain."

"Lack of pain doesn't necessarily mean you're not putting stress on your mind," Taylor said.

"As in, my brain might still be lighting up like a Christmas tree?" I asked.

"Something like that," Taylor said.

"I'll be fine," I assured him. And I wasn't lying. Not to him, or myself. It was a refreshing feeling.

"Good, because I think we may be dealing with something or someone unfamiliar," Taylor said.

"Do you think it's a Lost?" I asked.

"I think it's more likely to be someone from the supernatural community," Taylor said. "I think Rider would have noticed by smell if it were a Lost."

"Not all smell different," Rider said. "But you are right, these people smell human."

"That, coupled with what happened when they stole the witch's artifact, I think we're facing someone with powers I'm not familiar with."

"I've never worked with magic or anything," I reminded him. "I'm not sure I would know if I saw magic using my power."

"We don't know if it is magic, but if it is, you have a better chance than the rest of us of at least sensing something coming," Taylor said. "Even if you can't stop it, a warning will be useful."

I rubbed my hands together and stared out the window. It didn't sound like the best plan since it meant me seeing something I wasn't fully convinced existed. Even owning Frank, the idea of magic was foreign to me.

Taylor drove through the park. Large spans of forest surrounded us. It was beautiful in the dying light. I watched for a minute before closing my eyes and meditating while I still had the chance. My soul needed to be as aligned as possible. The entire plan unsettled me, but I couldn't say for sure why. Still, as a Reader, I would make myself useful, and I might learn something new.

Neil directed us to the driveway of the supposedly abandoned house. Taylor slowed to a stop, parking far enough down the drive to effectively block their escape. The only way these people were driving out is if they can drive through trees.

"Rider, we'll give you fifteen minutes to get into place," Taylor said.

Rider slipped silently out of the van and disappeared into the now dark forest.

Taylor twisted in his seat. "How far away are Jonathan and Angel?" he asked Neil.

"They, like, got stuck behind," Neil said. "They're just now getting the chance to leave."

"Stuck?" Taylor asked.

"Yeah man. The witches showed up. They knew their artifact had been stolen. Angel and Jonathan had to chill the situation down, but they're on their way."

"Even if Angel's driving, they're at least thirty minutes away," Taylor said. "Hopefully, this doesn't take us that long."

Once Rider's fifteen minutes were up, we quietly exited the vehicle leaving Neil alone.

"Is he going to be okay by himself?" I asked.

"As long as no one circles around," Taylor said. "We can't be sure they won't."

"There's a car coming," Neil said on our comms unit.

Taylor slowed. "What are they doing?"

Neil was silent for a moment. "Never mind. They didn't slow down."

"Good," Taylor said. "I'd hate to get boxed in."

We continued on, listening intently for anything out of the ordinary. We kept to the overgrown road, and didn't encounter anything unexpected.

"Do you know how far away this is from the portal stutter?" I asked in a whisper.

"According to Neil, it took place not far from here. It can be easily reached by foot."

"Is there any way to know where they're trying to open a portal to?"

"Not that I'm aware of," Taylor said. "I doubt it's anywhere good though. Or at least whatever it is they want to pull through wouldn't be."

My forehead creased. "How do you know?"

"If they were bringing over refugees, they would have contacted MyTH. We can generally help with those types of requests. If it was someone trying to get home, AIR would have been involved. There's nothing illegal about a portal, depending on how it's created of course."

The road opened up into a wide space with tall prairie grass interspersed with weeds. There was one car and no other signs of life.

"Can you tell where they went?" Taylor asked.

I took a deep breath and reached to the Path. A beautiful tapestry of color greeted me with only minor spasms of pain. The trails leading away from the vehicle were obvious.

"They didn't go to the house," I said. "And they have our artifacts."

The relics left a Path far brighter than people. The strength wasn't surprising considering the amount of power the arti-facts soaked up over the years. A bread knife would leave a trace on the Path if moved. These objects pressed blazing trails of fire into the Path.

"It looks like they've been in the house previously," I said, studying the area further. "Not today, though."

"Lead the way," Taylor said.

We kept our voices as low as possible as we continued on.

"Do they have all the artifacts with them?" Taylor asked.

"It's too hard to tell," I said. "If they were being carried separately from each other, I'd know, but they're grouped together. I could pick apart the Paths and find out, but it would take ages and I don't think this is the time."

"You're right," Taylor said. "There's only two reasons I can think of to take the relics into the woods. At least if they're staying at the house."

"They're using them, aren't they," I said, not bothering to give him the chance to continue.

"It's possible they're taking them out to hide them," Taylor said. "But I'm not sure why they would. Especially since they have more than one relic. If they were hiding these, there would probably be at most two left unhidden. The thorn and the witch's vial."

"What do we do if they open a portal?" I asked.

"Let's hope they don't," Taylor said. "It didn't work the first time. If we take away their power source, they shouldn't be able to hold open a doorway to another world."

"I'll keep the Paths of the artifacts away from the portal as much as I can," I said. "If there is a Path fueling what they're doing, I'm sure I can stop it." We walked silently, hoping we were catching up to our thieves and murderers. "They've stopped," Neil said, breaking through our comms again. "What the--" Neil broke off.

Taylor froze, then he fumbled to open a channel. "Neil!" Taylor hissed.

"I'm here," Neil said after a few moments. "There was like, a noise outside. I didn't see anyone, though."

"Are the doors locked?" Taylor asked.

"I'm not a child," Neil said.

"Are they locked?" Taylor snapped.

"Yeah man, they're locked."

Taylor shook his head and if I only saw his expression, I would assume he was fuming. The Path told a story of the fear Taylor felt. It was a deep-seeded fright you get when thinking the worst could have happened to a close family member. Taylor didn't move on right away and as I watched, his Path lessened in intensity until he was ready to continue.

At least I wasn't the only one in need of some sort of meditation to feel centered. Neil appeared to push enough buttons for Taylor to need for some inner harmony.

CHAPTER
TEN

Deeper into the woods, voices ghosted through the trees and seemed to come from more than one direction.

"I am behind them," Rider said so quietly I barely heard him through the comms.

"Can you see what they're doing?" Taylor asked softly.

"They are arguing," Rider said.

"How many?" Taylor asked.

"There are two people," Rider said.

Taylor paused. "We'll hit them from three sides to capture."

"That sounds like a plan," I said, hoping it happened as easily as Taylor made it sound.

We crept up and before long we heard the bickering. I ignored the argument and kept an eye on Taylor who made hand gestures. Two weeks ago, I wouldn't have been able to understand more than one or two signals. Thanks to Boone, I was fairly confident that I needed to stay still, while Taylor circled around.

I nodded. Taylor started to circle the small clearing.

"There are other people coming," Rider said.

Taylor hurried back to me and we slipped further away from our quarry before we risked talking.

"They are near the house, but moving in this general direction," Rider said.

Who else would be out here? "Were these people at any of the crime scenes?" I asked.

"I do not think that is the case," Rider said. "The new people spoke about tracking and then split up."

"How many of them are there?" I asked.

"Three," Rider said.

"Are they searching for us or for our thieves?" Taylor asked.

"I could not tell," Rider said. "It could have been either."

"Dude, what if the witches, like low-jacked their vial just like I did?" Neil said, surprising me through the comms. I had forgotten he had been listening in.

"The last thing we need is civilians out here," Taylor said. "Let's take the thieves into custody before the newcomers catch up to us."

"Same plan?" I barely got the words out. Pressure began to build and my stomach twisted causing me to wrap an arm around myself.

"Are you okay?" Taylor asked.

Fighting the urge to be sick, I nodded. "I am, but we have to hurry. They're opening the portal."

I wasn't sure when the two stopped arguing, but there was no mistaking the pressure that built around us. The contents of my dinner wanted to escape, but I kept my hand over my mouth, willing myself not to get sick, and followed Taylor.

We reached a spot where Taylor decided was the right place. He was quieter the first time he tried to circle around, but we were pressed for time.

I counted to sixty and moved forward, hoping I didn't count too fast or too slow.

As I approached the small clearing I saw the shell of the dimensional portal pressed into the Path. Large beads of power streamed through the air, circling faster than a gnome on speed. The portal hadn't opened, but the hole had begun boring through the area between the worlds.

Momentarily I thought about Vincent. What happened between the worlds when a new portal broke through? Could he be hurt by something like that?

"Dammit!" hollered the man. "It's another portal. This isn't what we're being paid for."

My attention homed back in to the task at hand.

"I told you this is the wrong place," the other man snapped. "If a portal opened once, it's likely to again."

"These are the coordinates we were given to break through," the first man said.

"Not anymore," the other man snapped.

"Well, shut it down before it takes all we have," the first man said.

They aren't trying to open a portal? If not that, what are they doing?

"Stop!" Taylor yelled. He walked out of the woods with his gun raised. Across the clearing from me, Rider did the same.

"Who the hell are you?" the first man yelled.

"Step away from the portal," Taylor said, ignoring the question.

I stepped out from my hiding place, making sure they knew that Taylor and Rider weren't alone. And, although I had my gun in hand, I didn't aim. I had more important things to deal with.

The relics fed the portal, keeping the bright lights spinning and pressing through to the other side.

"AIR," sneered the first man. "Get lost. This doesn't concern you."

"Hands up!" Taylor yelled.

I tuned the others out and concentrated on the items of power. Their strength blazed in the Path, but not as strongly as moments ago. Their Path faded, dimming a bit each second. Physical distance might be the best way to cut them off, but with strangers running around the forest, I didn't trust my ability to pick them up and run away unnoticed. Knowing my luck I'd take the relics and run straight into someone else ready to steal them.

"Cassie," Taylor called. "Can you shut it down?"

"It's going to take me some time," I said. "But I can."

A shot rang out and the first man fell. My concentration broke and I stopped, stunned as I watched the man drop.

"What the hell was that?" I asked, my voice entirely too squeaky.

"Get down," Taylor snapped in reply.

He moved to the fallen man, keeping his head down. The other man yelled and began to rant and cry.

Rider grabbed the hysterical man and dragged him to the ground.

More than anything I wanted to meld into the shadows and disappear, but I had no idea where the shots came from. And worse, the portal stood in front of us, fully open.

"Dude, AIR has the portal on radar," Neil said. "There's all sorts of chatter."

Taylor pushed on the injured man's chest. Finally, my brain kicked into gear and I dropped, getting out of the line of fire. Hank would be pulling up satellite imagery of the area. I had to shut the power off. Fast.

From my spot on the ground I concentrated on the objects

and their connection to the portal. To everyone else, the link would be invisible. To me it blazed like daylight.

Rider let out a dark, menacing growl. From his inner depths, a murky green Path emerged and rolled away from him.

It felt primal, but I let the sound and Path roll over me, making a mental note to later explore this new Path Rider had created.

Instead, I kept my focus on my work. Since I couldn't physically take the artifacts away, I had to stop them from feeding the portal.

Cutting the lines connecting to the portal was my best shot, but the harder I pressed down, trying to clip the cord between them, the more the power fought.

The energy of the artifacts had been released from its prison and it wanted to be used. Not want, as in a living consciousness, but as a natural force, the current searched for a connection and the portal was what was available.

What else did we have? There was each other, of course, but I didn't know what the ancient potential would do to something living.

I barely registered Rider jumping up and running into the woods. Taylor hollered at him, but I didn't let myself get distracted. They had their job, and I had mine.

Where could the power go if it couldn't go back to something living?

The only thing I could think of was the artifacts themselves. Grabbing the edges of the Paths I pulled them away from their current trajectory. The portal immediately slowed and winked out, although the marks were still obvious in the Path.

Then I looped the energy flow back on itself and into the artifacts, attaching them to themselves, one at a time.

I thought of it as delicate work, but that probably wasn't the right word. For me, the Paths were small and fiddly. When I grasped the artifacts individually, the Path tried to wiggle free. Taking my time, I took one strand at a time and anchored it securely to where it originated.

I began to sweat, but ignored my discomfort. It wasn't like I was weaving a tapestry, I was just looping the lines back to the source. And I sucked at it. Give me a wall of Path to smash into something any day of the week.

My sight became blurry when the task was almost complete. As I finished the last relic I cut myself off from the Path and fell back. Somehow, I managed to keep awake, but it was only a small comfort as I stared at the sky.

Mentally, a red flag waved around in my mind, trying to snag my attention. What had we been doing?

Gunshots. Oh crap. I didn't stand, but rolled over and looked around. Taylor's hands were bloody and he sat next to the injured stranger, but he no longer leaned over his patient. The other man was nowhere to be seen.

Neither was Rider.

"What happened?" I croaked.

"Are the relics shut down?" Taylor asked.

Shut down wasn't exactly accurate. "They're safe," I said. "Is that guy--"

"Dead," Taylor said, cutting me off.

"The other man?"

"Rider has him cuffed and he's taking him back to the house."

"What happened?"

"We aren't exactly sure. One of the three following us shot the man and according to Rider, they fled. Rider tried to catch one, but had to circle back to us."

I nodded, and didn't try to say anything else. I would have

loved to close my eyes and sleep, but a dead man lay a few feet away. It wasn't the best time or place to take a nap.

"Can you get up?" Taylor asked.

"I need a few minutes," I admitted.

"You're sure the artifacts are safe?" Taylor asked.

My forehead crinkled and I glanced over at the objects heaped together. "Sure. They're fine. I didn't pay attention to much while I was working, but the two we caught, they seemed surprised or upset that they opened a portal."

"The man didn't go into detail, but they were paid to open a doorway to another plane."

"Wouldn't that be a portal?"

Taylor shook his head. "Portals go to other dimensions. There are layers to our world and they were shooting for one of those."

"I'm not sure I understand," I admitted.

"There's no time for us to learn more," Taylor said. "Neil let AIR know that MyTH is near the portal, but they might still decide to send someone out. I need to get the vial for the witches and get back to the van."

"Just the witches artifact?"

"The others were reported stolen. The vial was our mistake. There's no need to get it wrapped into evidence."

"Worried about waking up as a frog?" I asked.

Taylor's mouth twitched up for a moment. "Something like that. Let's get out of here."

I looked at the dead man. "Get out of here?"

"I'll call the police as soon as you and Rider are on your way home."

"Home? Why am I going home?"

"You and Rider are switching out with Jonathan and Angel. From there, you're getting well away from this place."

"Shouldn't we wait and talk to the cops?"

"The moment your name appears in any law enforcement system, AIR is going to know. The last thing we need is to give them another reason to hold you."

"At some point I have to go to the Farm," I said.

"Not like this," Taylor said. "Trust me."

I smiled. "What are they going to do? Arrest me? I think a few of them are ready to anyway."

"Logan told you?"

I blinked at Taylor. "I was kidding. What are you talking about?"

"It's not important," Taylor said.

"It sounds like something important."

"You'll need to talk to Logan," Taylor said, standing up and reaching his hand out to me. "For now, it's time for you to go home."

THE IDEA of going home made my stomach twist. Home was closer to work. Being at MyTH wouldn't actually make me harder to arrest. For some reason, though, being at MyTH made me feel safer than my home.

Or maybe being at MyTH just made it easier for me to put the entire situation out of my head.

When Rider and I reached my house it was so late at night it was basically morning. I had planned on going straight in, taking a shower, and heading to bed, but the lights were on when we arrived, so Rider followed me inside.

Logan waited for us in the kitchen. I wanted to yell in excitement because he was back and all my worries of him being incarcerated could go away. But I also didn't want to wake Gran.

"They let you go," I said. My partner knew me well and I

was able to grab a fresh cup of coffee before joining him at the table. "How long were you stuck there?"

"Too long," Logan said. "I've made sure Kyrian is aware of my displeasure."

"Are you going to have to go in again?" I asked.

"They've warned me not to," Logan said.

"Warned you?" I laughed.

"Cassie," Logan said. "They're bringing you in."

I wrinkled my nose up as though smelling something bad. "They're going to keep me for ages to answer their questions, aren't they?"

"That's not exactly their plan," Logan said.

When he didn't say anything, I prodded him. "What is their plan?"

Logan looked down and twirled his cowboy hat around nervously in his hands. "Someone is going to be here at nine tomorrow morning to take you to the Farm. They're going to ask you some questions."

I stared at him blankly, wondering what my tired mind was missing. "That's not a surprise. They've been wanting to talk to me for days."

Logan still didn't look up. "After that, you're going to be a guest at the Farm until Vincent presents himself to an AIR office, proving he's alive."

My hurt sunk. "A guest?"

"They're holding off on a formal arrest, but if Vincent doesn't show in the next week, they'll bring formal charges," Logan said.

Rider put a hand on my shoulder which was nice, but I didn't feel comforted--I felt ready to strangle someone. Hopefully my boss.

"How could Kyrian let this happen?"

"You don't understand," Logan said. "In a week, they want

to transport you to a different facility. Kyrian is the one trying to stop that from happening."

Something caught in my throat. "A different facility?"

"It's a prison for the Lost."

"Are you kidding me?" I yelled. "That's crazy. It's ridiculous."

"I wanted to be the one to let you know," Logan said. His down-turned face was proof he didn't want to tell me at all.

"They cannot do this," Rider said. "Can they? There is no evidence."

"It wouldn't be permanent," Logan said. "There'd be a trial or something eventually."

"Trial?" It almost came out as a squeak.

"It will not come to that," Rider said. "Vincent will be back."

"Either way," Logan said. "You have until nine AM to decide what to do."

We sat in silence for a while.

"Do you want me to leave?" Logan asked.

"I'm not sure what I want," I said, trying to numb myself. "No, I take that back. I want a shower."

"Wait a moment," Rider said. "Logan, have you been at AIR this whole time."

"All day and into the night," Logan said.

"From the time you left MyTH have you been anywhere except the Farm?" Rider asked.

"I've been at home and here," Logan said.

"What is it?" I asked Rider.

"One of the men in the woods," Rider said. "The one that fired the gun. His smell is on Logan. It is faint, but there."

"An AIR agent shot our suspect?" I asked. "Someone we work with?"

Rider shook his head. "It is no one I am familiar with."

My brain was too full to add a mystery to the mix. "I have no idea what that means either."

"I'm in the dark here," Logan said.

"Rider will fill you in," I said. "I'm going to take a shower."

I left them downstairs. A part of me wanted them to stay, and a part wanted me to tell them to go, so I let my friends make up their own minds.

CHAPTER

ELEVEN

It was pretty hard to ignore the fact that I was getting arrested, but I had always been a champion at avoiding horrible thoughts.

Instead, as I showered I thought about my power. Aligning my soul seemed to be the solution to that problem. With some time, I might even be a better Reader. Rider could keep helping me meditate. When Vincent came back he could help as well.

Although, I wouldn't mind if Vincent and I did other things instead of meditating. It was hard to believe I was going to get a chance at having some sort of relationship with Vincent.

A real chance.

Rider was in my room when I came out of the bathroom.

"It's going to start getting cold soon," I said. "We should think about going somewhere warm this winter. We could take a vacation or something. You and Angel, me and Vincent, Logan and Hank."

"Do you think it is wise to make those plans?" Rider asked.

"Probably not. More than likely it's one too many couples

anyway. Besides, Vincent and I aren't actually together. Not really anyway."

The phone rang, but the readout was blank. My stomach squeezed tight.

"Do you think they made Hank take down the blocks on my phone?" I asked. Someone was going to come arrest me in a few hours. They probably wanted to check and make sure I'll be home.

"Logan did not say," Rider said. "But it is possible."

I took a deep breath and answered. "Hello?" I hated that it came out like a question, but the idea of being called by the people getting ready to arrest me wasn't exactly a comfortable one.

"Cass, it's me."

My eyes instantly teared up and I forgot everything. Vincent sounded tired and not quite like himself, but he was alive.

"You're back." It was a stupid thing to say, but I didn't know what words to use. So many cluttered my brain it was hard to choose. "Where are you? Are you okay?"

"I'm out west. Listen, I can't talk now, but I wanted to at least let you know I made it back."

A part of my heart fell. I wanted to talk to him. I'm not sure there was anything specific I wanted to discuss, but he sounded sharp and distant.

"That is Vincent?" Rider asked.

I smiled and nodded at him. Then Rider plucked the phone out of my hand.

"Hey!" I cried.

"Vincent, it is Rider." After a short pause, he added, "I am glad you are back."

I tried to reach for my phone, but Rider turned his back on me.

"You will talk," Rider said. "You must go into the nearest AIR office now."

Rider pursed his lips. "I am sorry, my friend. I do care, but it is not important right now."

I heard Vincent's raised voice and there was a sharp edge to his words.

Rider winced. "I understand, but Cassie is suspected of killing you. You will go into an AIR branch."

Vincent's voice came out rushed and loud.

"Don't tell him that," I snapped. "He just got back."

"Shh," Rider said to me. Back to Vincent he added. "I do not care how far away it is. Arrange something with Hank if you need, but you will go now."

My mouth dropped open. "Did you shush me? Give me the phone. Let him have some time to settle in. You can tell something is wrong."

Rider frowned at the phone, then passed it back to me. "He will regret it if he does not do this now."

I brought the phone to my ear, but I could tell I was too late. There was no one on the other end of the line. "Why did you do that?"

"I did it because he would want me to. I am his friend and I would expect him to do the same for me."

"We don't even know if he's okay."

"He will call back shortly. I am certain of it."

I wanted to be aggravated with Rider, but I couldn't be. It had been a week since I'd last heard Vincent, and now I'd have to wait longer without knowing if he was hurt.

But on the plus side he was alive and I wouldn't go to jail.

Thirty minutes passed and I my stress levels rose, but Rider didn't appear to be put off by the amount of time going by. In another forty minutes, the phone rang again.

I picked it up on the first ring. "Hello," I said in a rush.

"I've taken care of it," Vincent said. "Are you safe?"

"Never mind that, are you okay? What's wrong?"

"I need to know you're safe, and I'll be fine," he said in a tight voice.

"I'm okay," I reassured him.

"Let me talk to Rider for a minute before I go. I'll call you back in a few days."

"A few days? Why? What's wrong?"

"I need time." He sounded as though he spoke through gritted teeth.

"Okay," I said, sadly. "I'm glad you're back."

"It's good to hear your voice," he said. For the first time, he actually sounded like himself. "I'm sorry, I only need rest. I promise I'm not injured."

I smiled, feeling slightly reassured. "Thank you. We'll talk when you're up to it."

"Thanks, Cass."

I passed the phone to Rider, who looked nervous, despite having appeared unconcerned while we waited.

"Thank you," Rider said. "There was no way to avoid the rush." After a few moments Rider smiled again. "Of course. There is much we need to talk about, but it can wait until you are more yourself again."

A minute later Rider said goodbye and passed me the phone. Once again, Vincent was gone.

"He doesn't sound good," I said after a moment of silence.

"He does not. This may be how he is when he returns, though."

"It's possible. Is there food or water between the worlds?"

"We know very little," Rider said.

"Logan once said it was like Wonderland and hell all rolled up in one."

"Then it is no wonder he does not sound well."

"He's back, though," I said, trying to pull my spirits up. "That's the important thing."

"He is back, and the office knows it. Both are important things."

I smiled at Rider. "Do you think there will still be agents picking me up in a few hours?"

"I do not think so," Rider said. "There is no longer a reason to interrogate you."

"Think we should go into work today?"

"I think it should be avoided at the moment, if possible. Call Logan and let the office wait."

Want to read further?
Never-Ending Nightmare (AIR Series Book 8)

WRITING the AIR series has been a fun and amazing experience. There's more planned for Cassie and her partners!

IF YOU ENJOYED THIS BOOK, please leave a review on the site where you made the purchase. Leaving a review helps the reader and author in many ways. Your support is appreciated!

THANK YOU FOR READING!
Amanda Booloodian

COMPLETE WORKS

Complete works by Amanda Booloodian:

AIR Series (In Reading Order)
Stonecoat: Novella 0 (AIR Series Book 0)
Shattered Soul (AIR Series Book 1)
Redcap (AIR Series Book 2)
Broken Paths (AIR Series Book 3)
Stolen Sight (AIR Series Book 4)
Fenrisúlfr: Novella 3.5 (AIR Series 5)
Fractured Worlds (AIR Series Book 6)
Reliquary (AIR Series Book 7)
Never-Ending Nightmare (AIR Series Book 8)
Krampus (AIR Series Book 9)
Eclipsed Pathways (AIR Series Book 10)
Void (AIR Series Book 11)
Marked Soul (AIR Series Book 12)

AIR Series Box Set

AIR Series Books 0-4: Welcome to the Farm

AIR Series Books 5-8: Conspiracy Theory

AIR Series Books 9-12: Redacted

Spellbound Murder Series

Oath Bound (Spellbound Murder Series Book 1)

Grim Magic (Spellbound Murder Series Book 2)

Fallen Witch (Spellbound Murder Book 3)

Spellbound Murder Box Set

Spellbound Murder Complete Trilogy

AIR Series Audiobooks

Stonecoat: Novella 0.5 (AIR Series Book 0)

Shattered Soul (AIR Series Book 1)

Redcap (AIR Series Book 2)

Broken Paths (AIR Series Book 3)

Stolen Sight (AIR Series Book 4)

Fenrisúlfr: Novella 3.5 (AIR Series 5)

Fractured Worlds (AIR Series Book 6)

Reliquary (AIR Series Book 7)

Never-Ending Nightmare (AIR Series Book 8)

Krampus (AIR Series Book 9)

Eclipsed Pathways (AIR Series Book 10)

Void (AIR Series Book 11)

Marked Soul (AIR Series Book 12)

Spellbound Murder Series Audiobooks

Oath Bound (Spellbound Murder Series Book 1)

Grim Magic (Spellbound Murder Series Book 2)

Fallen Witch (Spellbound Murder Book 3)

About the Author

Amanda Booloodian lives in Missouri with her loving, and often times peculiar, husband. She has been passionate about the written word throughout her life. Now, much of her spare time is spent at the computer, delving into worlds accessible only through vivid imagination. In warm weather, when she isn't pounding on the keyboard, she can often be found wandering through the wilderness. Occasionally she gets it into her head to SCUBA dive or to sit back at home and make wine, which can have interesting results and inspire her writing.

You can find out more about Amanda and her writing, including upcoming releases, on www.Booloodian.com. You can also find her on Facebook: Amanda Booloodian - Author and Instagram: AJBooloodian.